CATACOMBS OF THE DAMNED

those who would steal living bodies in the quest for eternal life

P J CADAVORI

CATACOMBS OF THE DAMNED

those who would steal living bodies in the quest for eternal life

MEMOIRS

Cirencester

Published by Memoirs

MEMOIRS
PUBLISHING

25 Market Place, Cirencester, Gloucestershire, GL7 2NX
info@memoirsbooks.co.uk www.memoirspublishing.com

ACKNOWLEDGEMENTS

I would like to thank Memoirs Publishing for their support and guidance in helping me to produce this book. May I pay tribute also to William Shakespeare for his succinct turns of phrase, Chaucer for his story telling, Milton for his use of language and imagery and Livy, Tacitus, Herodotus and many other literary greats for their historical narrative. Not forgetting the greatest narrative of all time, the Bible, especially the Old Testament.

I have been inspired by more modern writers such as Thomas Hardy, Ray Bradbury, James Herbert, Anne Rice, John Connelly, Elizabeth Chadwick, Bernard Cornwell, Barbara Erskine, Michael Jecks, Rory Clements, Susanna Gregory and Manda Scott, along with others too many to mention.

PROLOGUE

His shaved head dominated an immensely brawny body which clearly begrudged being imprisoned within a shiny grey suit. His ample stomach and broad posterior seemed to be thrusting belligerently against the buttons and stitches in an angry attempt at freedom. His face was a bristling abomination of ghastliness, one you would never forget, though you would certainly try. The piercing, terrible eyes nailed down everything they saw, missing nothing, calculating remorselessly; a resolutely cruel expression of hostility. The bloodless face, gaunt and without a hint of mercy, provided the setting for a sensual mouth commanded by a savagely-hooked nose, like the beak of a large and brutal bird of prey. He exuded a vindictiveness which bred terrified silence in all who beheld him.

The bailiff. And he was knocking at my door.

'He's back again!' shouted Alison, who had taken refuge upstairs and was cautiously peeping through the side window.

'OK, children, don't answer the door!' I hissed.

So we stayed hidden, heads down, watching from the

windows. He was studying the front of the house with a glare that could have driven its way through a mortice lock. He turned and his eyes caressed the car with a look of sheer avarice. Finally he hunched his shoulders in defeat and we watched him stomp off back towards the road.

Then suddenly he stopped and swung around, obviously hoping to catch us watching from the top windows. He was clearly convinced that the house wasn't empty. He walked away to his car and drove impatiently off. We gave him 30 minutes, just in case he decided to wheel quietly back to catch us off guard.

We were a typically dysfunctional modern family struggling hard through mid-recession. My job had recently disappeared, which allowed 'more time with the family' and even more time to contemplate a cashless future. Yet at the same time, it presented the perfect opportunity to chase my personal, and admittedly rather selfish, dream of owning a country retreat.

We'd bought well in Notting Hill twenty years before; the house was now worth a bob or two. I reasoned that we could afford to exchange it for a bigger place out in the sticks somewhere and have enough left over to live in comfort, with a bit of luck.

'I AM looking for work!' I protested to Alison. But she knew better. She was not just my wife but my soulmate of countless years, going back to our schooldays. She was not easily fooled.

'Do you remember that lovely little village in Dorset we went to years ago?' I opened.

'Oh yes… Little Dancing?'

'Little Daunting.'

'That's the one.'

'Why don't we go and see it again, without the kids? You know, a weekend away from responsibilities, just the two of us.'

'It seems a long way to go for you to get your leg over in peace and quiet.'

'How…! well yes of course, that would be lovely…'

'Ah, that wasn't the idea, was it? I don't think you fancy me any more.' She pretended to be hurt.

'No no, it's just that I was thinking… we could see what sort of properties might be for sale around there.'

'Ah, now, miraculously, the truth appears, like a snake zigzagging from under a pile of rocks. See how it emerges, soundlessly, unseen and undetected.' Alison has a way with words.

'Er… yes, but less of the snake, thank you.'

We both laughed. Dorset beckoned.

CHAPTER ONE

'Bill, are you sure the children will be safe with those two in charge?' asked Alison nervously. We were standing in the hall, our bags packed for Dorset. It still shocks me how difficult it is for us to get away by ourselves. It was already spring, and with the bailiffs still lurking about the place our escape to the country was well overdue.

The children, Ben, aged ten, and nine-year-old Trixie, had insisted right up to the last minute on coming with us on the house search. They were now opting to stay put with Granny and our Romanian au pair, Vadoma, whose gypsy links, flashing eyes and anarchical attitude constantly inspired them to rebellion.

From up the stairs, Granny was glaring impatiently down at us. 'Hurry up, it'll be dark soon!'

'Yes, have good journey!' Vadoma was waving a little too enthusiastically, I thought. I couldn't help noticing Granny's conspiratorial wink at her.

'Bye! We're gone!' I yelled back, nudging Alison out of the front door and towards the car. 'They'll be fine' I tried to reassure her. 'I've hidden the gin where your mother will never find it. What can possibly go wrong?'

But I should have known better. Granny was over ninety and her bad habits were getting worse. She would gamble on anything, especially horses, about which she knew nothing. She picked them on their names, their colours, anything but their actual ability to run a couple of miles without falling over. And now the lottery was causing friction within the family.

'Remember when Granny practically killed Ben?' asked Alison.

'Yes, and he deserved it' I laughed. He had been entrusted with her lottery money to collect her tickets, but had come back several hours later with neither. 'Sorry Granny, no luck this time, I've checked them for you' he grinned, shamelessly sporting a new pair of trainers. She wouldn't get caught like that again. She had taken to checking every ticket herself with furious concentration, her head pivoting like a tennis spectator between the results and the tickets. And when she lost (a weekly event of high drama) she cursed everybody and retired with a bottle of gin to her lair in the crow's nest of the top floor, already with a gleam of low cunning in her eyes as she plotted the next week's numbers.

And she genuinely believed that Vadoma's gypsy background could be harnessed to help.

'But Vadoma gets on well with Granny, so I'm sure she can control her' I said hopefully.

'Huh!' from Alison. It's amazing how she can put so much into a word that isn't even a word.

Ten minutes later, we were approaching the Chiswick roundabout when Alison realised she'd forgotten her Rescue Remedy. 'It's no good, we'll have to go back. They won't have that sort of thing in Dorset.'

The house was quiet as we crept back indoors. Too quiet, perhaps. From the TV room came the faint sounds of cartoons. Well, at least the children were occupied. Alison called faintly 'Vadoma?' No reply.

We sneaked upstairs to the bathroom where Alison keeps her Bach flower essences. As we passed Vadoma's door, we heard Granny's chortle, followed by 'They never search in here. Gin helps my creativity you know.' Clinking of glasses. 'Bottoms up!'

Alison and I looked at each other. Did we dare push the door open a crack, or was that snooping?

We snooped. There they were, the conniving pair, curtains closed, Vadoma hunched over a circle of candles.

'Patience, Babushka, we will find your winning numbers. Long as you promise to share wins with Vadoma, okay?'

'Yes, anything you say, just get on with it dear.' Granny took a long swig of gin, rubbing her hands together.

'Numbers have magic, yes? We use ancient art of divination. We begin with your birthday, Babushka. March 10, 1920.'

Gently Alison closed the door again. She looked at me, then took a swig of her Rescue Remedy. 'I thought you said the children were safe?'

'Harmless amusements' I swallowed uneasily. 'Don't worry. We'll only be gone a couple of days.'

So, taking a deep breath and promising sacrifices to mollify the gods, we left them to it.

* * * * * *

The village of Little Daunting was approached down a steep and winding lane with rounded hills on each side. It was April, and winter was still in force. It was a grey, raw sort of day with low clouds and a warm drizzle falling. Not the best time to look at a new idea, but when you have a bailiff hard on your brush you can't afford to delay.

On the hills the grass was suffering from overgrazing, with no growth during the coldness of winter, and the forlorn horses, sheep and cattle gave it all an appearance of neglect. Along the muddy paths and tracks, puddles of dirty water stretched endlessly to the overhanging horizon, a merging of leaden dullness. The trees were generally bare with the rain finding no support, so the countless puddles were constantly growing, changing shape and merging in an uncontrolled riot of anarchy.

I rolled the old Mercedes estate to a stop to take it all in. There was a promise of spring in the pinky-white foam of the blackthorn thickets in the hedgerows, those bastions of year-round shelter which seem to line every lane in Dorset and Devon. Yellow primroses were beginning to stud the banks, and if you looked carefully in the damper parts where the hedgerows merged into woodland you could see the first lords-

and-ladies, their flytraps starting to emerge, a trial of temptation and death for small insects who get too close. The dog's mercury was starting to flower, a classical salute to the Greek god who discovered its healing properties.

'Vadoma and the kids will love this' I said hopefully. 'Poisons, medicine, lots of mud and puddles, as well as space for animals.'

'Perhaps' said Alison, reserving judgement. 'But we're not buying a copse.' Ever the pragmatist, my wife.

I climbed out of the car, stretched and looked at the scene around me. The bare ground was a blanket of fallen catkins, with the early violets and the pink flowers of the dead nettle giving flashes of colour to the greenness and the drizzling damp. The hoof marks of foraging roe deer stamped between the cowslips. I could hear an explosion of bird life and the harsh call of the pheasant. Skeins of geese and wild ducks were already searching the fields for the early growth. The woodland was busy with nesting birds, blackbirds, finches of many types, while magpies and jays looked opportunistically for unattended nests. Grey squirrels were searching everywhere.

I could imagine what a warm spring day would bring; bumble bees, honey bees, butterflies, dragonflies hovering over the wetlands, bright yellow celandines and the later flowering violets providing a rich food source. And a pandemonium of rabbits, foxes and badgers.

And so towards the river which bustled with new life; sticklebacks, newts, tadpoles all frantically living and growing while desperately avoiding predators like the kingfisher whose colourful tunic belies a harsh aggression. Myriads of water-boatmen, pond skaters skimming the surface, never resting. Water voles repairing the winter ravishes to their homes...

'Come on! How long is that pee going to take?' shouted Alison from the car. I got back in and fired the engine up for the final mile.

The narrow road took us past a row of small thatched cottages, with low doors, a small window either side and a row of three windows above with their old straw roofs playing host to a shambles of moss, weeds and greenery. There was even an ancient forge where the blacksmith was still at work over his glowing, flaming furnace. And so into the main green of the village.

Little Daunting was one of those quintessentially English villages where it seemed an outrage to bring in outsiders. We had cynically expected upended supermarket trolleys proudly displaying their crooked wheels, discarded takeaway cartons whiffling randomly in the wind and reappearing in the most unlikely places, crisp packets, carrier bags, bin liners, all struggling to be noticed and to be congratulated on their survival. Perhaps there would be discarded tyres, rubbish tipped in the hedges, even the stripped hulks of abandoned cars. But maybe this was a horror yet to come, a premature judgement of future sins because as yet there was none of this. Even to think of such a sacrilege, in such a setting, was like swearing before the vicar.

Before us stood the Bell, the village's smarter drinking establishment and the place we remembered so well from our previous visit all those years before.

'Look, that's the room we had' I said, pointing. Fond memories.

'We had to close the window' murmured Alison, a half smile on her face.

'Only because of the noise you were making.'

'Well we *were* courting.'

It was three o'clock in the afternoon.'

Alison giggled in that infectious way of hers.

The Bell's rival, the less pompous Green Man, faced us on the far side of the green. Between them were several large, square Georgian houses, punctuated by several sets of expensive-looking thatched cottages. On the green outside it were tables with umbrellas and beautifully-tended flower beds, all contributing to the idyllic pastoral scene. The village was even smaller than we remembered it, with no more than half a dozen shops including a baker, a Co-op, a newsagent, a beauty salon with two chairs and a fish-and-chip shop. Facing them was Little Daunting's greatest claim to architectural importance, a stately Norman church now dedicated to St George.

Clearly the most important task was to find a house which would give our family plenty of room for tantrums and door slamming, with spare rooms for guests. We had arranged to meet the local agent, a Mr Quentin Dawlish of Gurney,

Gurney and Dawlish, on the village green in front of the Bell. Mr Dawlish had promised us on the phone that he had a property up his sleeve which would suit us, but he had been strangely reticent about the details.

I was rather hoping he would be late and we would be forced to kill time over a pint in the lounge bar of the Bell, just for old time's sake, but the moment I parked the car on the gravel the door of an old Land Rover a few yards away slammed and a large and smiling man advanced towards me with a hand outstretched.

Mr Dawlish turned out to be a genial chap whose large head, fringed with wisps of grey, gave him a medieval sacerdotal look, above a drink-ravaged face with loosely hanging jowls. The purple nose, the weak, fleshy lips and the dimpled chin, all dominated by a roadmap of veins, spoke of many long evenings in the pub. His rotund form and wire-framed spectacles softened the impression by giving him an affable, Billy Bunter look. He looked sixty, but was probably much younger.

'Welcome to Little Daunting. Good journey?' Without waiting for the answer, he launched confidently into his spiel. 'I have just the place for you to see. It's a big manor house, but it's been empty for a while. The probate from the last owner's will took rather a long time to sort out, so many vultures swooping down to fight over it. But it's now free and on the market. And there's *no chain!*' He laid great emphasis on these words. 'So cash is king.' He gave an oily laugh.

'OK sounds great, lead on!' I said expansively, as if I was the kind of man who invariably had his pockets stuffed with fifty-pound notes. I caught an imploring look from Alison: *for God's sake try to behave!*

'But I must emphasise that it's been empty for rather a long time' said Mr Dawlish, ominously. He bade us follow him and strode off surprisingly rapidly along the green. I bounced along behind him, my eyes furiously scanning the view to see where he could be taking us. He had covered some two hundred yards beyond the Green Man (well within my MSD, or Maximum Staggering Distance) when he stopped, swung round, and gestured to his left.

There before us, set well back from the green, was a big square house of uncertain age, but probably last worked on (and certainly last painted) in Victorian times. The colourless, dusty windows gave it a forlorn appearance. Yet it was obvious that this house must once have been rather handsome. It was built of wonderful honey-coloured sandstone, with Boston ivy running rampant wherever its tendrils could reach, obscuring some of the upstairs windows and embracing the triangular gables under monstrously high chimneys. I could sense the bleakness of an unfurnished house, lonely and unloved. Yet it was a well-proportioned building which must once have been the envy of the village.

Mr Dawlish took out a large key and probed the lock. The heavy double-fronted doors opened inwards with an effort, hinges squealing in protest.

'Come, come, see what you think' urged Mr Dawlish. Alison hung back, her body language expressing her feelings all too clearly. I pretended not to notice and followed the agent's instruction. I stepped inside and she reluctantly followed.

The hall was high and dark, with bare walls decorated only by the ghostly outlines of long-removed paintings. At the far side was an ostentatious inglenook fireplace, anguished and desolate. I looked around. Several rooms led off the hallway, all identically depressing. Each had an empty grate and a large and ugly mantelpiece. The paint on the doors, walls and window frames was cracked and blistered. The bare treads of the spiral staircase were covered in a litter of refuse, old letters, papers and countless generations of beetle bodies, a few live and scurrying ones still among them. It presented a depressingly gaunt and haggardly lifeless face to the world.

Somewhere in the gloom under the stairs, something small and quick scurried to shelter; a mouse, or more likely a rat.

'I'm not going to pretend it's in *wonderful* condition' said Mr Dawlish gently, like a doctor saying 'I'm not going to pretend that a hernia is a *good* thing.'

We began to explore, taking a room each, then rejoining forces each time it threatened to become too much. Upstairs there was a warren of rooms, all as neglected and colourless as those downstairs. There was that desolation and desperation of careless solitude. The two bathrooms had cast-iron baths and basins whose colour, if they had any, had long been obscured by dust and dirt. Ancient cobwebs veiled the window of the main bathroom; loose strands drifted across the casement, stirring slightly as we entered, seeming to beckon to us.

'What's that?' said Alison sharply. The noise came again, a most peculiar groan from somewhere far below stairs, as if someone had been awoken unwillingly from a long sleep.

'Just the heating, I expect' I commented.

'There *is* no heating!' snapped Alison.

She stayed strutting around on the first floor while I followed Mr Dawlish in silence up the next flight of stairs to the attic, or rather a linked series of attics. It was all the same story. There were piles of dust-laden broken furniture and beds, cracked mirrors above drunken chests of drawers from which some of the feet had mysteriously wandered off, low sweeping ceilings merging into grimy walls, punctuated by poky, cobweb-blocked windows. Stray plaster had collected in filthy piles to add to the depressing and dismal atmosphere.

We returned, shuddering and with long faces, to the ground floor. The kitchen was large but predictably old, dark and bare, empty of the warmth of that 'heart of the house' feeling one expects from a kitchen. I had visions of disease-ridden rats growing bold, aggressively foraging with cruel eyes shining in the shadowy gloom, crowning vindictive white sharpness, jaws already grinding in anticipation…

We did not explore the cellars. The black hostile vault we could glimpse through the ill-fitting, ramshackle door was too much. Rising from that dark tunnel of cold damp air came a stagnant, oppressive and musty smell of decay, wrapped in darkness, deep silence and dust; and more dust. I shivered as the blackness seemed to challenge any intrusion; there was below us a sinister atmosphere of secrecy, wickedness and overpowering fear.

'As you can see, it has been a *beautiful* house' said Mr Dawlish ruefully. 'I know we estate agents always say this, but it really does have an awful lot of...'

'Potential' said Alison sarcastically.

'You're absolutely right!' said Mr Dawlish, entirely missing her tone. 'I do agree.'

'Thank you for showing us around' I said. 'I think we'll explore a little, perhaps have some lunch in the pub. I'll let you know what we think in a few hours.'

'I suggest the Green Man, not the Bell' he said confidentially. 'The Bell's been taken over by a chain. It's all eighteen-year-old barmaids in mini skirts who can't speak English and fifteen quid for a ploughman's served with mozzarella and kiwi fruit. And the beer's appalling.'

'Thanks for the tip' Alison said, her eyes rolling in horror at the thought of all those mini skirts. Nobody asked my opinion.

'There's one more thing I will say to you, and this really is between you and me' he added. 'I know the property is on the market for four-seventy-five, but I think it is fair to say that the owner might well be amenable to an *offer*.' Here he winked and made an exaggerated downward gesture with the open palm of his hand, as if pushing down the plunger of a cafetière. His meaning was clear; the price might well be reduced, perhaps very considerably.

The Green Man proved to be a cheerful establishment which at that time of day was littered in equal measure by tatty, well-thumbed copies of the morning papers and equally tatty locals reading them. Once inside, Alison let rip.

'I will not live in that house, however cheap it is! I don't know where to start. It's filthy, it has a horrible creepy feeling to it and it's probably haunted. And those are the good points! Do you want to hear the bad ones?'

Before I could answer, she was fortunately interrupted from the bar.

'Are you the people looking at the Old Manor? You've got a find there. Do you want to know its history?'

'Go on then' I said cheerfully.

He grinned, leaning across the bar. 'I'm Steve, by the way.'

'Nice to meet you. Bill Cavendish. This is my wife Alison.'

'It goes back an awful long way' he said, grinning.

'We're in no hurry. Oh, let me get you one.'

'That's very kind of you sir, I'll have a whisky if I may. Yes, many stories, very strange some of them. And you've come to the right man. I'm a bit of a local historian, you see.'

'Do tell us all about it' I said, with a mixture of excitement and an uneasy feeling of premonition. Alison was sitting with a glare on her face, pretending to take an interest in an old copy of *Dorset Life*.

'The stories go back at least four hundred years' said Steve. 'The really interesting stuff starts around the time of the Civil War in the 1640s. At that time witches and devils were a serious part of everyday life. In fact it was so bad that the Government appointed a Witchfinder General called Matthew Hopkins. By all accounts he was a very cruel man who was responsible for many innocent hangings.

'Now Matthew had a younger brother called Joshua, who owned and lived in the Manor. He was there for about forty years in the mid seventeenth century, and he was even nastier than his brother. He was a witchfinder too, but he was also a magistrate with a keen interest in alchemy, and as an extension of that, he was heavily into medicine.'

Alison sighed, rolled her eyes, folded her arms and stared out of the window. But she had put down the copy of *Dorset Life*.

'Joshua's great interest was hunting down witches. He would have them condemned in his own court and then hanged. The bodies were always disowned by their families, so he was able to use them for medical research, which was just what he wanted. He believed in one of the central themes of alchemy, that life could be renewed indefinitely with a sort of universal medicine. He believed that physical bodies could be rejuvenated, that they have a spiritual parallel, but you had to understand the physical body first.

'Apparently he dissected bodies. He did horrific experiments during the torture stage of getting confessions. He liked to cut out...'

14

At this point Alison got to her feet. 'I really don't want to hear any more about this. I'm going outside for some fresh air.' She shot me a look and marched off.

'I'll be with you in a moment, darling' I said. 'Sorry, you were saying?'

'No worries. Anyway, Joshua kept a mausoleum. Body parts. It was all recorded in his diary, but nobody knows what happened to it. And then the rest of the bodies, the bits he didn't want, were buried in unhallowed ground near the church. But that wasn't the end of it. The Manor was supposed to be the centre of a smuggling operation. The contraband would be landed in the estuary and then stored in the cellars. Joshua of course became very rich and was therefore untouchable by the law, although he used to hang the occasional smuggler to show he was doing his duty. He eventually died as a recluse, but there have been many rumours, and some say they have seen spirits from that time which still haunt the church and the Manor.'

'Why do you think they still hang around?' I asked, completely hooked on the story.

'The theory is that spirits like this are so traumatised that they are stuck here on earth. Maybe they want revenge in some form and just aren't able to move on to the spirit world. We really don't know why some stay around. It's said that they come back to haunt the house, to search for the diary and their body parts which were stolen by Joshua. There's supposed to be a hidden underground passage from the church and the catacombs which goes to the house.'

'Fascinating. But no one knows where it is?'

'No idea, apparently.' He shot me a sly look, and I wondered if he knew more than he was letting on.

'It would be a hell of a place to own. Good buy for you, I should think. They won't find many takers for a place that size round here.'

I left the pub deep in thought. I had no idea how I was going to sell all this to Alison.

Outside on the green, we sat and watched the ducks on the pond.

'If you think I'm going to live in that spooky, damp, depressing house you are completely mental' said Alison.

'I think it's fascinating. Didn't you like Steve?' I had seen the way she had flashed her smile when he had introduced himself.

'He has got nice eyes. Got the gift of the gab, hasn't he? But there's something about him I'm not sure about. Or the house.'

'Come on, it's superb. It's everything we've wanted. And this talk about ghosts and witches and things that go bump in the night is just so much rubbish, you know that. Then of course, if there really was an alchemist living there, we might find his pot of gold.'

'You just want a big house so you can make your friends in London jealous. So they can see how well you've recovered.' I had to admit that she had a point there. She knew me too well.

'Just imagine living in a house like that, though' I said gently. 'It's beautiful. It's huge. And you're right, it wouldn't half piss Caroline and Hugh off.' I chortled at the thought.

16

'Four hundred and seventy-five thousand pounds seems a lot of money to spend just to make my sister jealous' responded Alison. 'We could get a lovely modern four-bedroom house for that.'

'Don't be so boring!' I countered. 'Look, I bet we can get it down a bit. I bet we could get them down to four hundred and fifty, even less. That would leave us three hundred K for improvements. We could afford a decent holiday. You can go shopping, proper shopping. I'll take you to Knightsbridge for the day, special treat.'

'One day's shopping? Big deal. Tempting, and thank you. But really, come on!'

A shout came from the direction of the pub, and I looked over to see Mr Dawlish bowling across the grass towards us. His demeanour seemed more confident than before.

'Mr Cavendish, Mrs Cavendish! I've just spoken to our vendor. I have some *very* good news.'

'Oh no' muttered Alison. 'Don't tell me, he's found a charming little slaughterhouse that's going for a song.'

Mr Dawlish hovered on the grass, addressing us as we sat on the bench. 'As I intimated, they are prepared to drop the price very considerably' he said. 'If you felt able to offer say, four hundred thousand…?'

'That's very interesting' I said. 'In fact we were just discussing it. Could you give us a few minutes? Perhaps in the lounge bar in ten?'

'No! Not even at four hundred thousand!' said Alison as Mr

Dawlish retreated. But I could see she was weakening. We both knew that once it was up together, the house would be worth twice as much. And we knew the right people to do it, back in town.

'We'd have nearly as much again in the bank, Al. And it couldn't cost more than a hundred thou to do it up. It would be a wonderful project for you. Us.'

'Hmm. Two trips to Knightsbridge.'

'Three, if you like.'

'You're mad.' She shook her head in despair. I had won.

'I love you' I said, kissing her neck and getting to my feet.

I shouldered my way into the pub and saw Mr Dawlish hunched over the bar, talking in a low voice to Steve. He jumped up when he heard me come in, his face shining with hope.

'We've made some enquiries with our friends in the building trade' I lied. 'There are some serious damp and structural problems, as you know.' That part was not a lie. 'We would need to budget at least two hundred thousand on that place before we could even move in. We can make you an offer, but I'm afraid we are not prepared to go over three hundred and fifty thousand.'

A brief look of panic crossed Mr Dawlish's face. He thought for a moment. 'I am fairly sure' he said 'that I could persuade the vendor to meet you in the middle. Very sure, if you catch my drift.'

I was tempted to stand my ground, but I knew that at three hundred and seventy-five grand the Old Manor was one hell of a good buy. I was full of impatience to conclude the deal. And I knew I had now found the vendor's lowest price.

I marched triumphantly out on to the green.

'Done' I said. 'And twenty-five grand extra in the bank for a holiday. Or a racehorse, for that matter.'

'OK, well done' said Alison. 'I suppose. And Mum might like the racehorse.'

From the depths of her handbag her mobile began to chime and she dug it out from a pile of papers. 'It's Vadoma' she said, reading the screen. 'Hello? Vadoma? *What*? Slow down... who?... Oh no! Where were you? That's a disaster. We'll be back as soon as we can. In the meantime try to get him out of the house, and don't let him take *anything*!' She cut the call and hurled the phone back into her bag.

'We'd better get back fast' she said, getting to her feet. 'Somehow that bailiff got into the house. I couldn't get much sense from Vadoma, she sounded hysterical. And apparently Mum has disappeared.'

CHAPTER TWO

'Well, what happened?'

'Trixie let him in! I told her not to' accused Ben, sticking his tongue out.

'You didn't, you liar!' exploded Trixie tearfully. 'I thought he was somebody coming to buy the house.'

'Trix, we would have told you. Vadoma, where were you?'

'I help Granny on stairlift, she get stick stuck and whole thingamabob stop half way up. Take long time to fix.'

Granny looked a bit surprised, but nodded agreement from the safety of the top of the stairs. She was poised for flight if things took a nasty turn.

'This is what he left' said Vadoma. She handed me a paper listing the stuff the bailiff was laying claim to. Both televisions were on it, as well as our mahogany dining room table and chairs, the pine kitchen table, the sitting-room suite and Alison's car.

'He really rude! Say he come back in ten days to collect everything unless we pay before. His number here.' She pointed at the top of the sheet.

'Couldn't you have persuaded him...?' I began with a cheeky smile, but Alison caught me glancing at Vadoma's golden legs, currently rather freely exposed in a slit summer skirt, and gave me a warning look.

'OK, well, what's done is done. I'll call the agent to see what progress there's been with those buyers from last week. We need to get a move on.' Alison was already on her way to the kitchen, having decided that there was no sensible contribution she could make.

As we were talking, the phone rang.

'It's the agent' called Alison. 'The people last Tuesday, they'll meet our asking price. Shall I tell him to go ahead?'

'Maybe there is a god after all' I murmured. 'Yes of course. Come on everybody, let's go to Pizza Shed to celebrate and tell you about our new house.'

'Jimmy Watts at school says Pizza Shed is for losers who can't afford anything else' observed Ben caustically.

'Nonsense. We've always gone there. It's easy to park, and the wine is cheap for Granny. I am not lashing out for the petrol to go to Pizza Roma in Wymering.'

There certainly didn't seem to be any problems with the stairlift now, nor any marks on the wall as Granny abseiled down the stairs at her usual enormous speed.

'We want to tell you about the village' I said. 'We've found a house.'

'We can't move house!' protested Trixie. I'll have to leave Susanna and Amelia and all my friends behind. Anyway, the country smells of cowshit.'

'And pigshit, that's worse' said Ben, helpfully.

'And it's all mud. All my clothes will get ruined.'

'You can have new country clothes. We can have a puppy! And Trix, you can have that horse you've always wanted. And Ben, they have a wonderful cricket team. I'm sure you could get on the juniors' I ventured.

So, pushing everybody out of the door, I climbed into the old Merc and pulled into the traffic, the usual cloud of blue smoke marking our wake. The car would be the first thing to be replaced from the house sale surplus, unless our friend with the piercing eyes got to it first. Though come to think of it, he might save us a visit to the scrapyard.

Vadoma seemed enthusiastic. 'In my country we like countryside. Animals, plants, big haunted buildings, farms my family work on.'

'Haunted houses? Are there any castles?' Suddenly Ben took an interest.

'No castles, but the house is next to the church, and we've been told there are ghosts. And the blacksmith is next door, so he might want you to help.'

'Just like home' said Vadoma with a smile. 'And we make poisons from plants!' she added mysteriously. This made Granny perk up. 'Agatha Christie, dear' she confided. 'Wonderful plots. Murders. Great fun.' Her Shakespearean relish for cauldrons, witches and potions was a good match for Vadoma's love of the occult. No wonder they got on so well.

'I tell you stories from my country later. We have many

ghosts too' Vadoma said tantalisingly. She is convinced that God created gypsies because He found the world to be too dull, and gave them that wonderful talent for story telling, which always included a philosophy of life to prepare children for future trials and disappointment. In her world, love and hate are both embraced and entwined, being made equally welcome.

We arrived at the pizza place and of course there were no parking places, so we turned left into the narrow, dark street which led to the pay-and-display car park. Having parked, we walked back down the street, which was flanked by junk shops, a couple of estate agencies and a rather seedy bookmaker Granny pretended not to know about, until the louts lazing against the door waved and shouted greetings at her.

When we got there we found the place already buzzing with activity. There were about twenty tables, all brightly coloured with red and white check tablecloths. There was constant movement as waitresses scrambled between customers and the ovens. The kitchen was open to the restaurant, so there was always something to watch, and the bustle of talk resonated around the walls, amplifying the sense of noise and activity.

Suddenly Vadoma started waving madly at a tall, blonde girl by the kitchen, who waved back and came over. They embraced and started gabbling in some unknown language.

'This Marianna, my friend' enthused Vadoma. 'She work here and look after us. This my family!' to Marianna.

'Hi, I got nice seat, follow me' said Marianna over her

shoulder as she weaved towards a reserved table by the window.

'Yes, you certainly have' I murmured quietly to myself, watching her rear view. Unfortunately I didn't say it quietly enough, and Alison glared at me. I knew the usual lecture about being an old lech would be coming later, and my usual defence about being too old to change would be dismissed. But this was really just a formality we would go through. Alison is one of those lucky women who have managed to increase their allure as they get older, and has reached her mid-forties looking better than when we first met. Maybe she is slightly less slim than she was and maybe there are small signs of sagging, with lines starting around her mouth and eyes, but a lifetime together makes such changes happen invisibly. And I should admit that I may not be quite as slim or as fit as I once was.

'This your table' said Marianna, showing us to a large round one by the window.

'That's perfect' I said. 'Thank you. I hope we haven't taken someone else's?'

'No worry. I fix' with supreme confidence. 'We blame booking mix-up. Someone else's fault' she laughed wickedly.

She was one of those women you can't help turning to look at in the street; well, I certainly can't. Tall and elegant, she had natural blonde hair falling shoulder length around a perfectly symmetrical face with laughing blue eyes, dominating full lips with startlingly white teeth and a straight nose. She was wearing regulation black trousers with a soft mohair pink top which loosely followed the contours of her breasts and suited her looks perfectly. Yet, wonderfully, she seemed to be completely unaware of the effect she created around her.

'Two bottles of the house red, dear' jumped in Granny. She was a bit slow in many things, but drink was not one of them. She was an entertaining old relic, for all the wrong reasons. She rarely knew where she was or what day it was. She had made it through the invasive pestilence of radio, TV, aeroplanes and mobile phones and now faced bravely the infestation of the internet. 'It's like cockroaches, dear, once they've arrived you can't get rid of them.' She had been a part of the decline of Empire ('the Labour Government, don't you know'), and wobbled her skeletal body around talking in a confused string of *non sequiturs*. She looked quite ghoulish when she forgot her teeth, her cheeks sunk into the gap emphasising the alert, beady eyes above. Yet, I had seen photos of her as young girl which showed that she had once been rather beautiful.

'Yes that's fine.' I nodded to Marianna, who moved off, slipping between the chairs and some new arrivals who were milling around aimlessly. We settled down with the menus, after a battle as to who should face the window, and tried to edge as far away as possible from the wall-mounted speakers. The music was trying to be Italian, the waitresses were Eastern European, the food had been made in Germany and the crockery was from (but not of) China. What it is to be British.

'You like my friend!' observed Vadoma, winking cheekily. 'She visit us in new house now, she not like city. She country girl, might stay for long time.'

Alison just looked at me, words unnecessary.

'OK that's fine, we'll have plenty of room' I said, looking everywhere except at Alison, who doubtless would express some views about this later. 'I hope we get lots of our friends visiting. Kids, it's a big house with lots of garden to play in. And the village is safe so you can ride your bikes around. We have broadband so all your computers will work, and as a treat we'll get Sky so you can watch sport and nature programmes.'

By this time Marianna was back and Vadoma was telling her all about the move. In fact it was hard to interrupt the machine-gun exchange of jabber. She opened the bottle and asked me to taste the wine, even though it was a screw-top. But of course, she was only doing what she had been trained to do, by a leisure sector executive who did not know wine from bath salts. Switching languages seamlessly was yet another talent the children could learn.

'Just pour it please' I said. I ordered the necessary pizzas, with a spaghetti to allow for Granny's few remaining teeth. She'd much prefer a liquid diet, but her doctor didn't approve. 'I'm giving up doctors for Lent' she'd promise every year.

We spent the next hour batting our plans for the move backwards and forwards. It was a surprise to see how conservative and resistant to change the children were.

'They like routine' explained Alison, and Vadoma agreed, but began persuading them that travel and new things were fun. She drew a wonderful picture of a 'travelling' life, new places, new friends and no responsibilities, which really appealed to the children. We let them get on with it, while getting quietly sozzled, although Alison looked a bit miffed, mainly because she was driving.

'And don't forget the poisons' threw in Granny.

'Can we try them on Fatarse?' asked Ben, eyes sharp with excitement.

'Don't call him that to his face, will you. No, we won't be seeing him again unless we are very unlucky. But you can talk to Steve in the pub. He knows all the local legends, and how everybody in the graveyard died. Our house is just next door. We can catch rats. There are lots of outhouses, woodpiles and places where they like to live. We can go hunting for them, get an air rifle.'

So, an uneasy truce was agreed with the children, the first hurdle crossed. We would leave as soon as possible. We would be cash buyers, so it should be fast.

* * * * * *

And so the day of the removal arrived. The house was in turmoil, with boxes everywhere, the removal men were talking loudly while stacking up the two large trucks under the jolly supervision of an extremely well-fed chap with a clipboard. We were busily sorting stuff into piles – one for the move, one for recycling and one for the council tip. This last mountain was insultingly large.

'You're just in time to see us' Granny told Mr Clipboard.

'We'll be moving soon. You see all these boxes? They belong to the new people. I wish they would move them out of the way.'

'No Granny, we're moving today, these are all ours' said Ben. Mr Clipboard sidled away to safety, looking a bit surprised at Granny's contribution.

'Look out for the old girl' he whispered from the side of his mouth to his helpers. 'She could be dangerous.'

CHAPTER THREE

'I'm stunned' Alison said. 'Mr Dawlish has really excelled himself.' She was referring to the house, which since the time of our last visit had undergone a metamorphosis from neglect to superficial refinement. True to his word, our agent had marshalled an army of locals to clean up the main living areas of the house, tidy a path through the jungle, paint the windows and door frames and remove weeds from the brickwork. Even the front door had ceased to squeal in protest. And so the unpacking started, with Ben and Trixie immediately disappearing to lay claim to their territory.

Mr Bollow, the vicar, was one of the first of the villagers to float in, pushing his way beatifically through piles of boxes, luggage and crates. His welcome proved somewhat overwhelming. He had a rather fearsome approach, with his rotund belly, booming voice and a wall-eyed squint which rather conveniently allowed him to leer at the girls with one eye while appearing to be looking at the ceiling with the other. He was clearly a lecherous old goat.

Both Vadoma and Alison immediately saw which way the

land lay. These insights have always been a mystery to men. Perhaps he got away with it because most of the villagers didn't know which eye he was using. But he was an excellent vicar in one respect, because when things needed to be discussed the meeting was invariably in the Green Man (the church vestry being too cold, the vicarage itself being under the baleful eye of Mrs Bollow), which assured him a large and loyal flock.

'It's so nice to see some new parishioners, and what a lovely family you have' he said, beaming round at everyone. I was slightly insulted by the implication that Vadoma and Marianna were also my children.

'Lovely? Who's he talking about?' said Ben, looking around, genuinely mystified.

'We must sit down over a cup of tea soon and I can tell you all about the village' he went on.

'We're very keen to muck in and be a part of country life' I said, somewhat lamely. Ben and Trixie said nothing, but flashed their collective eyes to the ceiling as if to say 'speak for yourself, you old fart' and 'you? A cup of tea?' We had lived in the same house in London for ten years and never known our neighbours' names, so this immediate intimacy was rather alarming.

'No time like the present' enthused the vicar and launched into his life story, having apparently forgotten the original purpose of the visit. Or maybe he felt that the new owners of the Manor might have connections enough to help his move to a bigger parish through influencing the bishop. Eventually, quite by chance, he stumbled back on track.

'Yes I've been here for seven years now and I keep my eye

on all the village issues' he said. 'I would like to get your family involved with the church, as there are so many worthwhile things to do. You know, flowers for Sundays and special events, the fetes for Africa, the church roof fundraising events, the harvest festival. The list of useful things to do is endless. And the children can come to Sunday school and sing in the choir.'

'Can we go back to London please?' they shuddered in unison. Luckily he didn't stay too long after we asked him to help with the heavier boxes into the house, so we had the rest of the day to ourselves.

'Let's go to the pub for lunch, and then we can walk around the village' offered Alison.

'Can we see the blacksmith's first?' asked Ben. Vadoma was more interested in the church and the graveyard. Granny ominously wanted to look for plants, while Alison and Trixie wanted to see what shops there were. I felt an afternoon of 'research' in the pub was the best way forward. So there was lots to argue about at lunch.

We locked up as best we could and walked to the Green Man, a picturesque two-story thatch-covered stone building whose walls gave unwitting sanctuary to numerous small creatures in the rampant ivy. I had discovered that the pub was an old coaching house dating back to the dissolution of the monasteries in the mid sixteenth century. During that time most of the hospices were destroyed or sold off to prominent landowners, so alternative accommodation sprang up to provide food and shelter to travellers. The pub was gradually built on over the next hundred years or so to include a large courtyard and stable block at the back, which looked after horses and the stage coaches of the 17th century. A hundred years later, when the postal service started, there were further extensions. There was even a room set aside for the magistrates' court.

This was the heyday of the coaching inns, before the Victorian era got under way. Then the railways stole the road traffic and new inns built by the railway stations forced the decline of the coaching inns; they never really recovered. So the Green Man was just a remnant of a glorious past, its stables and outhouses long gone.

'Can you imagine the creepy-crawlies that live in there?' shuddered Trixie, pointing at the ivy. I am still not convinced that Trixie and the countryside will ever agree on anything. We walked in through the dark oak door.

'Bad luck to walk under a sign' Granny pointed out as the Green Man sign lazily swung back and forth in the breeze.

'No, that's ladders' whispered Ben. 'She's hopeless.'

'The Americans used to bring us stockings' Granny added helpfully.

'Yes Granny' said Trixie. 'What IS she talking about now? And look at that disgusting face on the sign, he's got things growing out of his mouth. Yuk!'

We wandered into the warm, square, brightly-lit wood-dominated bar area and I breathed in the comforting smell of beer. The bare wooden floors supported about twenty large round tables, each circled by wooden rustic chairs with brightly-coloured cushions. All of this was dominated by a bar with copper foot rests which ran the whole length of the back wall, behind which were row upon row of bottles.

'Why are some of those bottles upside down?' asked Ben. 'Are they for Australians?'

'Good morning, welcome back' said Steve, leaning on the bar. 'Move going well?' He was looking at Vadoma, who was wearing a bright red low-cut top.

'Yes, we've met the vicar already.' I introduced everybody. Vadoma seemed to be as interested in hearing more about the church and graveyard as Steve was in telling her. Granny started to take an interest too.

'I can show you around that when I'm off this afternoon. But what can I get you now?' asked Steve.

The menu produced an immediate source of conflict with Trixie.

'I want pasta' she said. 'What's with all these pies – rabbit, ugh! And what's toad-in-the-hole?'

'Oh yes, wonderful horse, won at Aintree, 1955' enthused Granny. 'Or was it Mr Toad? Hundred to eight and the favourite fell at the last.'

'We can do you some pasta' said Steve.

'Hmm. Bet it's horrible' Trixie looking sulky at being caught out.

When eventually wine, gin for Granny and food for us all were sorted out and we were starting to relax into the normal family disagreements, a large woman sailed across to our table like a galleon under full sail.

'Steve tells me you are the people moving into the Manor' she boomed, in a voice which would carry over a battlefield. 'I'm Mrs Fairley-Dyer. My friends and I cleaned up the house and garden for you. It was quite a job, I can tell you!'

'Hello Mrs Fairley-Dyer, thank you so much for all you have done, it must have been such hard work' gushed Alison. There were introductions all round.

'We can't thank you enough for all your work. I didn't recognise the place' I added.

Meanwhile Mrs Fairley-Dyer was waving at her friends to come over. More introductions. Three more bottles of wine. The country might turn out to be more expensive than I thought.

'I do hope Mr Dawlish told you about the deathwatch beetle?' Silence. It took a while to absorb that one.

'I've heard of those things. They make a ticking noise when it's dark and quiet, don't they? Well, I'm sure with modern insecticides we don't need to worry…?' My optimism was clearly lost on Alison. She looked at me. Words were not necessary.

'We had a huge fire in the garden and everybody in Little Daunting was there' said Mrs Fairley-Dyer. 'We burned papers, stripped off all the wallpaper. Some of the furniture was simply riddled with woodworm, I'm afraid. It was quite a party.' At my expense.

'Woodworm *and* deathwatch beetle, I'm surprised it hasn't

been made a nature reserve' observed Alison, her voice dripping with ice.

'I do like a party' perked up Granny. 'When is it?'

'Well, these are all things we will have to live with' I told Alison, trying to give off an air of confidence and knowledge which I clearly didn't possess. I don't know why I bother. Alison said nothing; sometimes her silences are worse than words.

And so lunch rumbled on, two bored and grumpy children, the women giving us all the good news about the house's defects, Alison getting more and more withdrawn. I felt overwhelmed with problems which I thought I had left behind in London. I was finding out that city problems have country cousins which are different but just as virulent.

Only Vadoma seemed to be in her element, talking to Steve. We found out later that he was filling her head with stories of horrors, ghosts, torture and murders from the civil war days. The Manor seemed to have been in the middle of it all.

'There is passage from the house, goes into church basement' Vadoma relayed to us. 'It goes through the catacombs, Steve says. But nobody knows where it is. Catacombs are where they keep dead bodies.' She now had the full attention of us all.

'Wow! Can we go and look for the passage?' asked Ben.

'I don't know. We need to ask Mr Dawlish. Somewhere deep down below the cellar, no doubt. But let's walk around the village now. We can start with the blacksmith.'

The blacksmith worked in a square brick and flint cottage set back from the road. A dark brown-red tiled roof covered four upper windows painted in the traditional way with opening sections in white and the outer frames in black. A double 'stable door' stood in the middle with the top half open and the bottom latched. A porch surrounded the door, decorated with old-fashioned roses and brightly-coloured clematis which was climbing randomly, dropping tendrils of flowers over the edges. In front was a small cottage garden with more roses blooming happily alongside wilder and more uncouth invaders such as the blues and pinks of milkwort and campion. All was surrounded by a three-foot-high flint wall with a white gate hanging half open in the centre.

We could hear the dull clang of a hammer pounding metal, so we cautiously pushed past the gate and walked the ten yards or so up the cinder path. Looking over the top of the stable door we found a Hadean nightmare of fire, heat and molten metal. The room was surprisingly small, with floor tiles of ancient granite upon which stood a large iron anvil at waist height, over which a flat piece of glowing metal was being shaped.

The smith, a tall skinny man with grey hair wiring out at all angles from his scalp, was dressed in a tattered leather apron. He was surrounded by a mass of tools and discarded iron bars. There was an old gate in the corner and a huge furnace blazed in the centre of the back wall. Next to it was a large shovel, and a pile of coal and wood contributed to the dusty and volcanic atmosphere. The heat coming off was so fierce as to deter entry. But Ben, eyes wide, pushed past and went as close as he dared.

'Hello there! Stand back while I finish this' said the blacksmith in a deep, smoke-distorted voice, which was however friendly.

'Come back Ben' said Vadoma as sparks flew off the red-hot metal. The smith dropped the bar into a tank of water to cool it down, producing an explosion of steam.

'You must be the new family at the Manor?' he opened. It seemed everyone knew who we were.

'Yes, we're looking around, getting our bearings' said Alison.

'Can I try?' interrupted Ben.

'Not today young man I'm afraid, I need to finish this. Next week I'll be shoeing some horses so you can come and help me then.' He looked at me for agreement. I nodded gratefully; anything to get the children happily integrated.

'Come on now, we need to leave him to work. Let's go and look at the church.'

'Steve says he will show us around when he finish pub' said Vadoma.

'OK, so if the door is open, let's just take a quick look around and wait for him.' We walked gingerly into the graveyard. Even on this fine day it carried an air of menace. Everywhere we looked we saw old, lichen-covered stones leaning at drunken angles, most of the inscriptions illegible after many decades of rain and frost damage. It appeared that this graveyard had simply been left to rot, along with the bodies interred within it. The subsidence over the centuries as the earth had settled into the chambers below had destabilised and in some cases toppled the gravestones. Yawning caverns could be glimpsed below some of them, and it was hard to miss the faint musty smell coming from below, a chilling contrast with the bright summer fragrances above ground. Ben knelt down and peered inquisitively into one of them.

'Do you think the bodies have all rotted away?' he asked seriously.

'Oh yes, long gone, don't worry about that' I reassured him, though I think he could sense the lack of conviction in my voice.

Ben kicked at a loose stone and watched it slither into the earth below one of the gravestones, which was inscribed 'Isaiah Williams, 1801-1844'. It landed with a hollow thud. His eyes widened in astonishment.

'I hit a coffin!'

'Nonsense, it was probably just a… tree root or something. Come on, come away from there, it's dangerous to get too close.'

In the newer part of the churchyard one or two grand graves, obviously belonging to the titled or wealthy, were surrounded by newer ones in black granite or white marble. Ben looked at them thoughtfully.

'This one says Marjorie Carstairs, nineteen twenty two to nineteen ninety-eight' he said. 'I bet she's not even a skeleton yet. I bet her flesh and her hair and her skin are all still there. Do you think if you dug her up she would look just like…'

'Stop that now! It's disrespectful!' snapped Alison. 'You're as bad as your father.'

'Sorry Mrs Carstairs' said Ben.

We pushed open the heavy oaken door into the church, and no sooner had we stepped inside than we heard steps behind us. 'Hi there!' said Steve, breezing in. 'Isn't this church amazing? It goes back to pagan times. There was a sacred site here which the Saxons built over, and when the Romans came they changed it again. That was followed by Christianity. I often imagine the satanic battles for the soul which must still go on in the afterlife! But what you see now is mainly the Norman structure. Just imagine all the intrigue, all the killings which have gone on here over thousands of years.'

Alison shivered, but Vadoma was staring around the church wide-eyed, as if she could see again the scenes of brutality which must have been played out here in centuries gone by.

We walked through the porch and down the nave, which was covered by a braced roof supporting the vertical arches. Near the top was a row of clerestory windows which signally failed to let much light in and could perhaps help to explain the gloomy atmosphere. At the end of the nave was an ornate wooden rood screen which separated the choir from the main body. It led into the intimacy of the chancel, where a very simple altar was erected. Turning around and looking down the nave, we could see at the other end the inner stairway thrusting up the perpendicular tower where the organ and bells were housed. The only stained glass was above the altar. The other windows were unvaried and monotonous in their white light.

Alison shivered again. 'I need to get out' she said. 'There's something here that doesn't feel right.'

'Yes, I feel it too' said Vadoma.

They were both mesmerised by the same thing. It was a huge mediaeval mural about fifteen feet long and ten feet tall, split horizontally across the middle by what seemed to be a bank of clouds. Above the clouds was a host of angels and mortals in the traditionally joyful garden of heaven, while below was a scene of complete horror. There were hideous representations of animals and of tortured and agonised people in various stages of punishment. Fire and heat blazed under a ladder down which naked sinners were tumbling to hell from the upper part of the mural. The lower section was all emblazoned in lurid red, ochre, yellow and orange. The sufferers' bodies were drawn into that world, their legs powerless to move away. And close by, the stone font contributed with more Norman designs of hell. In the corners stood vast, threatening monuments to families long since departed, effigies and gargoyles with faces to inspire terror. It was really not a very friendly church.

'OK, come on Granny, we're leaving now' I said, to break the spell.

'Oh good. Are we going to the pub for lunch?'

'No Granny, we've had lunch.'

'But we can't leave now, Steve says there's still lots to see, the basement leading into the catacombs' protested Trixie, who was now starting to take a morbid interest.

'OK, we can come back another time. We need to see the rest of the village. But I am NOT going down there!' shuddered Alison.

Leaving the church, we turned back towards the huddle of shops behind the pub. I felt a sense of relief to be in the light again after the oppressive dark horrors which had seemed to threaten us and will us to let them loose, as if they were pushing against invisible restraints.

'I must give you a quick look at the Old Barn' said Steve. 'We use it for village meetings, it's the polling station too. It's an architectural mixture going back centuries.'

We found the Old Barn behind the vicarage, down a short and narrow lane. The long wooden structure with its beautifully-maintained thatch roof was a compelling addition to the nearby buildings. 'It's owned by the church, so it's well looked after; certainly better than the graveyard' Steve added.

Inside, the earth floor stretched uncluttered down the whole hundred-foot length, with huge ancient cruck-style beams horizontal and vertical, producing a tunnel-like effect. The sides were constructed with weatherboarding and split oak pales, with ventilation slits at regular interval. At the top was a nesting hole for a family of barn owls, no doubt encouraged as the resident rat killers.

'Hey, this is cool!' said Ben. 'We can play here.' There were stacks of hay bales against the walls. 'We can make houses out of these!'

'It's really quaint' said Alison. 'But I still feel uncomfortable here.'

'There has been much horror here!' Granny announced. 'Great suffering. I remember it well, you know.'

'Don't be silly Granny, you weren't born when all this was happening' I chided her. We only found out later that during the Civil War the building had been used as a place of judgement and execution.

We left the barn and walked around the various small shops, the Co-op, the newsagent, the baker's. It looked as if we would be pretty much self-sufficient.

'So here you have it all. Except for the gypsy encampment at the lower end of the village, down by the river' said Steve. 'I'd better get back to work. Maybe see you later?'

'OK, thanks for everything Steve. It's been really interesting.' It was time to go back to the Manor to sort out more boxes.

'Next week we'll go and look at the school, it's an old converted abbey' said Alison.

'But you told us we wouldn't have to go to school if we came here!' Trixie was always testing the boundaries.

CHAPTER FOUR

The gypsy encampment hovered uncertainly in a semi-permanent state at the far end of the village, down on the river flats. It was much talked about by the other locals, but seldom visited. In winter it was usually surrounded by river water and rancorous mud which seethed and bubbled quietly, ready to capture wanderers who strayed off the paths. The whole area was littered with an assembly of junk and rubbish, featuring rotting wooden crates, collapsed barrels with staves awry and jumbled piles of scrap iron colourfully rusting in twists. There was a general aura of neglect, decay and idle abandonment. And when the winter morning mists would villainously merge with the pungent reek of the river mud, an overwhelming sense of dank fearful horrors lurking for the uninvited would assail the senses. It was as if the rejected filth was forming an alliance, to hover for vengeance against those more fortunate.

Stories abounded in the village of the characters living there, down to rumours of witchcraft, child theft and cannibalism as well as more mundane accusations of dishonesty and shiftlessness. The integrity of the clan was said to be paramount, with all outsiders a target. We had been warned about the encampment, but Ben and Trixie wanted to see for themselves.

'They must need friends if no one likes them' said Trixie charitably.

'But don't worry, we won't go there Dad, it's too dangerous' said Ben reassuringly. He was hoping to put my mind at rest, but the way he was looking at Trixie told me he intended precisely the opposite.

When the two of them disappeared the next day we decided to call Reggie, the local bobby. Reggie was a gentle fellow who liked people rather too much to carry out the more stringent aspects of his job. In his simple outlook there were no shades between right and wrong. But then perhaps such an uncomplicated character is, after all, ideally suited for the job.

'I'll go look for them. Fonso is the leader, his wife is Esmeralda' he said. 'Children are safe with them though, I wouldn't worry.'

'But we've heard stories about child theft, children vanishing into slavery' I worried. 'Perhaps I'd better come with you.'

So we drove as far as we could, then left Reggie's Land Rover. 'I bet it won't be in one piece when we get back' I muttered. I knew all about gypsies, or thought I did. We climbed over a stile and set off over the fields on a gentle downward slope to the settlement.

The area housed a gaggle of caravans, temporary lean-tos and muddy paths betwixt and between. As we headed towards

Fonso's caravan, suddenly, rushing out of a lean-to, hurtled Ben and Trixie, huge smiles on their faces.

'They are really nice people, we've had such fun!' bubbled Trixie. Then Fonso and Esmeralda appeared. Fonso looking darkly malevolent. His eyes looked as if they had witnessed much evil, a depraved product of an early life in the brothels and bars of waterfront dens and knowledge of vices beyond imagination. Until he smiled, when his warm, brown eyes displayed a kindliness and an intelligence I had not been expecting. Esmeralda was large, colourful and cheerful, the perfect serum to Fonso's looks.

'They can come here any time' she said, looking defiantly at Reggie.

'Morning Fonso, morning Esmeralda' from Reggie. 'All OK with you? Children all going to school every day? I hear yours are doing well.'

'Do you want to try a cup of my gypsy tea?' asked Esmeralda, looking pleased to hear a compliment.

'A real privilege' said Reggie. Suburban London had ill prepared me for this.

'Thank you, sugar and milk please' I said, immediately feeling guilty and regretful. Esmeralda yelled 'Florika, get some milk, and take it out of the clean bucket'. Florika, who looked about Trixie's age, quickly arrived with a mug of milk, which she poured into my tea.

I couldn't believe that Trixie was now drinking out of a plastic mug which just a few days ago would have been demoted to the trash bin. Her eyes sparkled with enjoyment and she was whispering to Florika, both girls glancing at me and giggling. But then Florika was one of those girls who could sell anything to anyone. She had an innately attractive face with even features, framed by dark hair which fell to her shoulders and shone with health and vitality. Her light grey-green eyes had an oriental hint, with wonderful depths of calmness and character.

Next to them, Ben was chewing on what appeared to be a piece of wood. Our children had found life and friendship in a most unlikely place.

'Thank you for looking after them so well' I said. 'We're new to the village. It's really wonderful that they have found friends so quickly.' Little did I know where that friendship was to lead.

We arrived back at the car to find the Land Rover intact but with an old gaffer leaning on the bonnet, propped up on his thick shepherd's crook, the handle polished from long usage, gripped by distorted and gnarled knuckles. But his wrinkled face was one of quiet calm with generations of tranquillity from working the land.

'G'mornin Varmer Zalter' from Reggie.

'G'mornin Reggie. Oi don zee yer very auf'n, oi tell yer retoired like gen'l vokes?. Yerd tell ole vicar lorst 'is 'orse. Oi tol' ee zee thee 'ee be proper twily an' crowting'

'What is going on?' I said, completely mystified. The children looked on with amazement, eyes wide.

'This is Farmer Salter who farms over the Spinney way' said

Reggie. 'He tells me the vicar is complaining because he's lost his horse.'

'Vicar zed ee disappeared, vanished loik las' week's wages. No volks zeen 'ide nor 'air of en. But er bist chaynee-eyed so maybe miss un. Oi tol' ee stick up rayward nowtiz for rayturnin.'

'Chell zee vicar loikely' said Reg, obviously fully bilingual. 'Lookee yer, this yer be volks in Manor, chillern wantin a 'orse, could ride about plaaces visitin. These gypsies 'ave un for 'unned poun. Very purty too.'

'Caw bless my zaul. Zounds loik vicar's 'orse. They'm a bad lot mind, condiddle everythin."

'Oh aarh, oi better zee to 'ee, and what all bezides. Oi be win 'ee dreckly.' Reg translating this as 'The gypsies' horse might be the vicar's which was stolen. I'll have to look at this.'

Ben said 'that's cool, I want to talk like that.'

Farmer Salter looked at the sky, licked his lips and said 'Oi loik a guddle to Green Man. Yerd tis unhealthy to work 'tween meals' hinting broadly.

'OK, we can take you there' I said, looking questioningly at Reggie. 'We can fit him in the back' suggested Reg. I was completely at a loss for the whole conversation as Farmer Salter squeezed in the back with the children.

'Oi dunno wher' yume gwain to sit to, but squaize in there someplace. Thee be roight angletwitch.' Said the farmer to Trixie. *They've brought us to a foreign country, I'll never see my friends again*, Trixie was clearly thinking.

We soon got to the Green Man, where Farmer Salter and Reggie scrambled out for several 'pipevuls of baccy and quarts of zoider'. 'Laafin' loik maad they were' said Ben, already picking up the vernacular.

'Caw, 'ark at 'ee' said Varmer Zalter. 'E be roight Dorset.'

'OK, come on. We need to get your mother and look at the school. Then we can go to the RSPCA centre to see if we can find a dog.'

'Yes!' shouted the children in unison. 'But do we have to go to the school?' added Ben.

So we returned to the house, picked up Alison and went on to the school. We drove through the outskirts of the village and at the end of a long drive found a huge confusion of ancient rambling buildings in an extensive open landscape of about a hundred acres, dotted with games pitches. There was a large car park directly in front of the main entrance with a porter's office just inside the gigantic, heavily-carved wooden doors. The Headmaster, Mr Fernyhough, was told we'd arrived.

'Welcome! I understand you've now made the move since we last spoke a few months ago?'

'Yes all done and dusted. The children are looking forward to starting school.' The said children glowered silently.

The head took us on an extensive tour of the ground floor and showed us a vast array of classrooms and common rooms and a huge assembly hall next to an extremely well-equipped library with canteen facilities at the far end of the west wing. Up a beautifully winding marble staircase was a far-flung array of dormitories for the boarders, interspersed with teaching staff living accommodation and many large rooms dedicated to staff offices and tutorial rooms. In all, it was a building to get lost in with ease.

'We assign a second-year pupil to all new children for two weeks to help them acclimatise' said Mr Fernyhough. 'They take similar classes and share the same break facilities, which helps the newcomers to settle in. We take great pride in trying to produce excellence in academic achievement, while balancing it with sports, travel and language skills. We have a real mix of pupils, from wealthy local landed families to bursary and scholarship children from poorer backgrounds.'

'Does Florika come here?' ventured Trixie.

'Of course not, Trixie!' I snorted *sotto voce*.

'She certainly does' said Mr Fernyhough. 'She's one of our brightest bursary children. She studies science and biology. Would you like her to be your guide?'

'Oh yes please!' That was Trixie sorted.

Vadoma was speechless. Such places were just a dream in her country.

Eventually we piled back into the car and drove through the village to find the narrow, winding lane to the RSPCA centre, where we had been told there was a large facility for strays.

'Can we leave Ben here?' Trixie suggested.

'No, we'll leave YOU here!' instantly from Ben.

'Now stop that, both of you!'

We could hear the barking from about two hundred yards, and pulled into an empty car park. We checked into the reception and were shown into the main compound.

Nothing had prepared us for what awaited. There was row upon row of cages, each containing the supplicating eyes of another abandoned and homeless mutt. Desperation, despondency and helpless appeal flooded out on us from all sides. Big brown eyes spoke of pain, suffering, neglect and rejection. Tails wagged in frenzied appeal.

Vadoma and Trixie were visibly upset. Alison managed as usual to bolt down her emotions, knowing a businesslike approach was called for, even amidst this deluge of mournful baying, howling, whimpering and yapping.

Ben immediately took a liking to an enormous German Shepherd with a huge head, open mouth and lolling tongue between outsize teeth. He had a dense coat of matted black and brown fur and bright, intelligent eyes. Only his slinking posture rang alarm bells.

'Someone has not been kind to poor Rufus' said Tracey, the girl in charge who was a lesson in emotional control and toughness to us all. 'But he has a lovely nature. If you do give him a go and he doesn't fit in you can bring him back'.

'Oh now look at *you*' I heard Trixie coo, and joined her to find her making friends with an oddly-named but lively-looking mongrel called Muffin, black and reddish-tan and one of those dogs with a tail so energetic that her whole body vibrated. She looked up with huge appealing brown eyes, and Trixie was lost.

It was all I could do to drag everyone away. We left the dogs for a two-day 'thinking period', having been told we could collect them if we still wanted to after that time. Both children were in tears at leaving their new best friends behind, while Alison delivered a lecture about animal responsibility. Which nobody listened to.

'Why can't Muffin and Rufus come with us? You're all so mean.'

So a dog-free, morose and gloomy carload arrived back at the manor to be met by a slim, forlorn figure with long blonde hair sitting on the front door step. Marianna from the pizza house.

'Something wrong!' cried Vadoma, who immediately got out of the car and ran over to exchange hugs. She was closely followed by Alison, thankfully always able to meet and resolve a challenge. Marianna started crying and there followed several minutes of explanation with Vadoma in a tone of voice which was so expressive that Alison was already guessing at the cause.

'Marianna got nowhere to go. Bad man follow and chase after work but she escape, get hitch lift' explained Vadoma with a real sense of outrage, looking as emotionally shocked as Marianna.

'It was very clever of her to find us' said Alison. 'Well, she must stay here now. We can give her lots to do to help her get over it.'

As usual, her down-to-earth practicality was swinging into action. All of this was watched by Trixie, eyes large, vaguely starting to comprehend the dawning of adulthood which was creeping, unwanted, into her life.

CHAPTER FIVE

The trouble began quietly, at first. It was a few months later, after one of the vicar's meetings, when we began to sense a slow, insidious infiltration of fear into our family, and into the village itself. It was a filthy night, although nothing out of the ordinary, and pouring with rain as we all tumbled out of the Green Man to sprint 200 yards to the Manor.

Mr Bollow was coming into the pub, leering horribly and shaking water off himself like a large and clumsy dog. He had just finished a 'prior meeting' at the Bell and was filled with religious fervour for the next one, again nothing out of the ordinary, this enthusiasm for meetings being an inspiration to civil servants worldwide. He trod on Rufus (yes, we got the Alsatian), who gently sank his teeth into the ecclesiastical calf. Mr Bollow bellowed like a banshee, which started up several other dogs. Suddenly the old-fashioned juke box was eclipsed by a clashing crescendo of pandemonium, an orchestral descant of chaos.

Finally calm of a sort descended, though it was full of

recriminations. We escaped and struggled home through the monsoon, trying to avoid Ben, who always takes joy in leaping with both feet into the largest puddles and then getting upset if there is nobody close enough to drench. Horrible little boy. Perhaps he might improve by the time he gets to forty.

Then it was back to the old house with its moods, its mystique of strength and timeless longevity. Tonight it seemed to be shaking in the gale and almost vibrating on its foundations, though the hugely thick walls stood firmly anchored. The house seemed to be responding to the howling of the storm, the deafening peals of thunder, the tumult raging over the roof, the uproar screaming around the gables and chimneys, and the rain driving in sheets and battling against the windows like hail, furiously assaulting the gaps in the building but unable to penetrate. It was as if the house was rejoicing in its primeval strength with this struggle of eternal proportions.

We all arrived simultaneously and pushed rudely through the back door, dodging the old-fashioned fly papers cloaked with bodies hanging from the kitchen ceiling, to be met by Marianna. She had fitted in perfectly from the moment she had arrived, and her grasp of English was already ahead of Vadoma's.

'Ben, take off your boots! I have cleaned the floor. I not know who's worse, you or dogs!' she shouted as she emerged from behind a curtain of drying clothes hanging from a rack, suspended from the ceiling by a worn rope which constantly threatened to collapse and create piles of further mayhem. She was wearing a loose-fitting top and a pair of very tight-fitting jeans. We were still celebrating our newfound sense of wealth after selling so profitably in London and buying so cheaply in Dorset, and both Vadoma and Marianna had felt the benefit when they had joined family shopping trips to Yeominster.

'Woof woof!' barked Ben cheekily, sticking his tongue out as he made his escape and falling over Trixie as they both tried to get through the door together. They were making faces and laughing insanely.

We still knew almost nothing about Marianna's history and strongly suspected she had no right to be in the UK, but she had taken to us as we had to her, and she did not seem to mind the cold, damp and general decay in the house, nor the requirement to do her share of the housework and cooking. She had spent a productive two hours carrying buckets, plastic containers, saucepans and anything watertight to catch the drips from the ceilings in a variety of rooms.

'And don't trip over the buckets, you can help me empty them tomorrow' she said. The children silently vowed to disappear when that rewarding task threatened.

Marianna had proved to be a blessing, helped as far as I was concerned by the fact that she was extremely easy on the eye, though she had learned to dress down a little when going out so as to avoid distracting the attention of the male locals too much and irritating Alison. She had taken to wearing her hair up and her skirts long, like a starlet dressed as a schoolmistress in the opening scene of a porn film, and wore make-up only for visits to the pub or for shopping trips. But she and Vadoma had proved wonderful, albeit eccentric, additions to our household.

It had taken us a while to realise that Mr Bollow's frequent visits were less from a sense of pastoral duty to us than to a desire to leer obliquely at both Vadoma and Marianna whenever he could, and at Alison too if he had the chance. They had taken to teasing him by praising his smart ecclesiastical outfits or laughing at all his comments as if they were profoundly witty. He would bask with pleasure in their supposed admiration.

As we returned from the pandemonium outside, having achieved some semblance of order inside, we suddenly remembered that it was time to check that Granny was still with us.

'Trixie, go and make sure Granny's OK please. Her room is cold and it leaks' said Alison.

'Aw! I don't want to.'

'OK, I'll do it' said Vadoma cheerfully. Up the stairs in the semi-darkness she ran, with much stubbing of toes, heaping colourful Eastern European curses on whichever government it had been which had foisted energy-saving bulbs on to us.

She had a huge rapport with Granny, a strange attraction between women of completely different backgrounds. They had several points in common. Granny too was of uncertain age and had been born in an obscure corner of the empire where record-keeping and other fundamental things were either unheard of or had been destroyed in a tumultuous orgy of independence. Vadoma used to compare this with post-Russian Eastern Europe. There too, anything applying to the old regime was dismissed as no good and any replacement was assumed preferable. This caused great consternation to civil servants, who, in the absence of basic records such as birth certificates, had to approve Granny's entitlement to medical care and a pension.

Even agreeing that she legally existed was a problem, as seeing her for themselves was apparently not sufficient proof. The local health authority once had to take her to hospital, where the staff were not quite certain who she was and delivered her back to the wrong house. Unfortunately the Tesco delivery van was there at the same time and the shopping was thus given some extra variety. Delivery check: 2 hands of bananas, 1 topside of beef, 3 iceberg lettuces, 1 granny.

'Who ordered the granny?'

'Nobody here, we already have one. Can you take her back please?'

Eventually she had arrived back home to report that she had met some lovely people, but she must have been late because she had not been offered a cup of tea. 'Although there was an ambulance there, so perhaps somebody was ill and they were too busy.'

'Yes Granny, but you're home now.' Dotty old thing.

She has long been a favourite with the children, going back to their earliest Christmas memories. The joy of wrapping up a small parcel of rotting fish-heads and other unmentionable horrors in bright and cheerful Christmas wrapping paper, and then dropping it on the pavement to see who would pick it up. Watching from an upstairs window and seeing strangers stopping to examine the road, the wall, the overhanging tree while attempting to look like the vicar, with eyes swivelling downwards in a most unnatural movement while simultaneously checking out who was watching them. Seeing no witnesses, they would swoop down to collect the surprise and bear it off in triumph for later examination. So far not one of these packages has ever been handed in unopened to Mr Bollow's Children in Need programme, so charity at Christmas appears to be a myth.

Granny normally preferred to keep to her own domain up in the attic. She zoomed up and down on a stairlift we had installed for her, but generally preferred to stay upstairs, with regular forays into the cellars to 'keep an eye' on things generally, and the bottles specifically. Just the previous evening, Granny had clearly had one of her adventures into Hades. She had something rather obviously concealed under her dressing gown.

'Granny's got a bottle of gin' accused Trixie.

'I'm sure she doesn't really' said Marianna diplomatically. That earned a needle look from Trixie, who recently got a lecture from the school about telling porkies.

But Granny moved with amazing speed, her stick clack-clacking down the passageway to the back stairs and her escape route on the stairlift. She felt safe up there as the noise was deadened by dust, and ugly trunks and dark furniture crouched in piles to attack stray children. Dark, threatening shapes jostled soundlessly for precedence, shuffling forward to be the first to pounce. Even the old piano with its black and yellow teeth hovered as if about to attack.

When the children had friends around, it became a matter of honour and bravery to lead a fearless expedition among the lurking terror. 'Last one to go in is a cissy' whispered Ben, so young James went home early to avoid being humiliated for the rest of the day.

Granny could hear them creaking up the stairs and lie in wait. After taking a few steps into the cavern she liked to snap the lights off and groan in a most alarming and terrifying manner, followed by much screaming and yelling as the children fell over themselves to escape. She could then get stuck into the gin in peace and continue to sort out, classify and catalogue her herb collection.

This was the scene which met Vadoma when she pushed the door open, hinges creaking as if to preserve its privacy. Granny's main living area, her 'laboratory' as she called it, was a large room, cool and dark, which smelled of dust, ancient leather, wood and musty, dried flowers, all jostling to compete with the exotic smells of rosemary, juniper and a bewildering variety of woodland plants. On the uneven bare boards there were open bookcases bulging with books, magazines and papers, long library tables whose surfaces were practically invisible beneath the tangled confusion of leaves, jars and branches, and shelves against each wall groaning with the weight of yet more collections. A large antique desk with a leather top supported yet more muddles but was dominated by what looked like a fox's skull. Beside it were three bulky armchairs worn with age, the cloth hanging in shreds from the arms where unknown generations of fingers had enlarged the holes.

The low ceiling was supported by heavy, dark beams with bunches of herbs suspended from every space, while bulky support posts disappeared into the roof. A small cobweb-encrusted window overlooked the church, and this, facing the prevailing wind, gave vent to many frightening noises during storms. It was too high to reach from the outside, so the climbing plants were free to decorate the windows and their tendrils would tap on the glass to produce an eerie noise whenever the wind blew.

The last time Vadoma had gone up into the attic she had come down looking rather distracted. She had complained that she had felt a strange coldness, a clammy embrace which had caressed her through her clothes, rather as Mr Bollow always did with his eyes. Drawing on countless generations of gypsy lore, she had shrugged off the feeling and gone through to Granny's lair.

'There's something up there' she said later to Alison, 'something that is not at peace'. Alison looked puzzled, but not entirely surprised.

'Are you OK, Babushka?' shouted Vadoma, pulling her jumper closer.

'Yes, come in dear.' Granny was leaning over the big desk in the centre of the room, sorting out dried plants. 'I'm putting them into categories, you'd better help me. I'm just working on the poisons.'

Vadoma's eyes lit up - Nirvana indeed. She looked around and saw stacks of dried plants everywhere. In the far corner was a large number of jars, a mortar and pestle and several containers for distilling and cooking on Granny's old-fashioned electric stove. This was the 'simpling' area, where herbs were brewed and distilled.

'Yes, we need all this equipment' said Granny. 'These jars are for steam distillation, which breaks down the walls of the cells to release the plants' essences. These jars I use for ointments. I boil the plants to extract their ingredients and then make them into a paste. See all these connecting pipes, labels, sieves, the grater? I've got all the equipment, you know.'

There was also a glass fish tank which was alive with woodlice, plastic bags full of dried horse dung to extract the ammonia, and bottles of vinegar for preservation.

'Put this over there, with the others' Granny told Vadoma as she passed over a handful of vegetation.

'What is this?' she asked, admiring the purple bell-shaped flowers which hung from a straight green stalk.

'Ah yes very poisonous! Belladonna, my dear, deadly nightshade. It grows in woods. Put it there by the yellow one. That's henbane and the long spiky one is digitalis, foxglove. All very poisonous. There are many plants we need to save. Do you see that tall one, like an umbrella? That's angelica. We keep it with the mistletoe and valerian because it's a defence against witchcraft.'

'Yes we have those in my country too' said Vadoma. Her eyes were wide and her mouth open as she absorbed the scale of Granny's efforts. There were piles of nuts for spells, divinations and poison antidotes. There were branches of hawthorn and elder, favourite allies of witches.

'It's all organised into areas' Granny went on. 'Medical cures, curses, portents death and disaster, flowers to encourage fairies. Look, that's ragwort. It hides fairy treasure! And my sacred book of trees is very important. One day we'll need all this, mark my words!' she added ominously.

Vadoma shivered. The temperature seemed to have fallen further. She felt a peculiar sensation; icy droplets of cold sweat seemed to be trickling down her back. There was definitely something strange in the attic; an underlying disquiet and anxiety beneath the placid veneer of normality.

CHAPTER SIX

It was yet another wintry, rainy day when the vicar telephoned to say he would be dropping by later that morning. He wanted to talk to us about some strange goings-on in the village, and to see if we had seen or heard anything, or indeed if we were having similar experiences in the Manor.

He always gave notice of a visit because he lived in mortal fear of Rufus, who, sensing his unease, would react accordingly to emphasise where he stood in the pack's pecking order. In reality Rufus and Mr Bollow got on remarkably well when he was not standing on the dog's tail, as did Muffin (yes, we capitulated entirely to the children's demands and Muffin too had become part of the family).

When Marianna first arrived the vicar came bursting through the back door in a huge state of excitement. Someone had told him she came from Transylvania, so perhaps he thought there might be vampirish influences which would need exorcism. This was one of the more imaginative reasons for an afternoon leer, but he caused a complete breakdown in law and order as both dogs, showing complete contempt for the clerical collar, exploded into a chaos of noise. Our Transylvanians dashed frantically around shouting and trying to control the pandemonium, and making more noise than both the dogs. After calm was finally restored we took mugs of tea into the drawing room. Trixie and Ben were there, to learn manners, although they rudely, and loudly, always ran bets on the vicar's eyes when Marianna, Vadoma or their mother were in the room. When Vadoma, in one of her low-cut tops, leaned forward to pour the tea, the vicar's eyes popped out in a most alarming fashion.

Muffin, who was always partial to black labradors, would innocently sidle up to the clerical leg and start schmoozing; apparently black trousers and shiny black shoes are more than a girl can resist. So Mr Bollow, while trying discreetly to push her away, had to balance his teacup while leering through his ear. And Trixie and Ben start arguing about who owed whom for the revolving eyes.

Invariably the children were sent out to play, usually making a bee-line to the kitchen where the 'daily', Lynn, was normally baking. Ben had been known to remove the dead flies from the flypaper and poke them into the cakes. Last time the vicar came around he complimented Lynn on the freshness of the scones, and said the currants were particularly soft and juicy. 'No currants in they, Mr Bollow" responded Lynn in a puzzled voice.

Rufus had quickly settled in, convinced that he was the alpha male. He had managed to learn how to open the room doors with his front feet, so we had to replace the horizontal door handles with round knobs. He stunned everyone on one occasion by charging down from the attic, opening three doors without breaking stride and going straight out to the garden to annihilate a squirrel which had unwisely decided to dig up some bulbs. The squirrel fled, and Rufus returned to plop himself in front of the Aga and look coyly at Marianna as if to say 'Aren't you lucky to have me to protect you from being ravished by those fierce squirrels?' She ignored him which just encouraged him to further excesses.

It was Rufus who startled the vet one day by howling for hours with a grossly-extended stomach. It turned out he had helped himself to a whole box of Weetabix.

So later that day, Mr Bollow turned up with Gavin, the owner of the Bell. After the usual welcome from the dogs, we settled into the drawing room.

'You know Gavin's barmaid, Penny?' asked the vicar. 'Yes, of course you do. Well, this has only started recently. Penny says that when she walks home past the Old Barn every night she hears voices.'

'Yes, Granny does that after a bottle of gin' I joked. This earned me an old-fashioned look from Alison. But Mr Bollow did not notice.

'She told Gavin and he went to have a look.'

'I had a look inside, but there was nothing there' said Gavin. 'But she says it's been happening for some time.'

'There do seem to have been an awful lot of strangers moving around the village recently' the vicar went on. 'They are definitely not tourists and they don't seem to have any connections here.'

'Yes, it's all a bit strange' said Gavin. 'They come into the pub, keep to themselves. They always drink cider and seem to be unfamiliar with our money, so I have to help them out. The last one a few days ago looked haunted. He had the coldest blue eyes. There was a darkness about him, an atmosphere of evil.'

'What did he look like?' I was intrigued.

'He wore a bulky blue knee length overcoat, which he kept tightly closed, with heavy working boots covered in mud. Even though it was a warm day. And when he left I looked out of the door to see where he was going, he had completely disappeared. There was no sound of a car, and he couldn't have walked away so fast. It's all a mystery.'

'And Mr Dawlish?' prompted the vicar.

'Yes, when old Dawlish got home on Tuesday night he found his house had been trashed. He called Reggie but they could find no sign of forced entry. No windows broken, no doors forced. But inside it was chaos. All the crockery in the kitchen was lying broken on the floor, all the drawers in the house had been emptied, cupboards ransacked. But there was no theft. His cash, credit cards, all the electronic stuff was untouched. It was almost as if they were looking for something specific.

'Anyway, last night I got home at about midnight and as soon as I walked through the door I felt my house had been – well, violated. It was a ghastly feeling. But nothing had been touched. There are rumours going around the village, and they're getting stronger. It's like a mass fear, an uncontrollable hysteria.'

'The whole village is talking' added the vicar. 'Everyone seems to be talking about odd happenings.'

Vadoma, Marianna and Alison looked at each other. They had all experienced various degrees of discomfort lately, but had thought nothing of it. Until now.

'Yes, we are feeling these things' said Vadoma. 'In the attic where Granny lives, is not good, not nice feelings.'

'When I went down to the cellar last week I couldn't wait to get out, I don't know why' said Alison. 'Just a weird feeling that there was something behind me, over my shoulder.'

'Have you spoken to the gypsies yet?' I asked. 'They're supposed to be able to understand these things. Maybe Vadoma should go there with you. With her Romany background she might see things we can't.' I was deeply suspicious, as I had no feeling for this sort of mumbo jumbo.

'Yes, I go with Steve' smiled Vadoma. 'He knows them there.' I could never entirely understand the fondness Vadoma and Marianna shared for our barman. But as Alison had said, I suppose he did have remarkable eyes.

It took a while to walk down to the gypsy encampment. The fields and paths were deep in mud and Vadoma had to keep stopping to collect plants for Granny, but nevertheless it was exhilarating. It was a cool day. A slight breeze was shunting fluffy clouds across a blue and white speckled sky, but the threat of rain coming in from the more ominous, bruising cloud banks in the south west gave some urgency to what could easily have slipped into an aimless stroll in the country.

Startled hedgerow birds bolted at our approach, while a buzzard soared above the fields looking for prey; this was reward enough for the long walk.

Eventually we arrived at the outer caravans of the encampment. We stopped to look across the river at the old mill on the far bank, long disused, and to wonder at the beauty of the estuary waters. It was an area where several small rivers met and embraced into a larger main channel, with swamps and wetlands on each side. I knew the slow-moving, crystal clear water was home to a huge variety of wildlife; salmon, trout, pike, minnows and large eels, the favoured prey of the otters which were often glimpsed at dawn or dusk. Above the water a crowd of damselflies and dragonflies were teasing the kingfishers which had nests in holes in the riverbanks, competing with water voles for the best sites. The lush vegetation of purple loosestrife, yellow iris, water mint and reed grass, lilies and pondweed was all moving gently in tandem with the water and the breeze. The huge green leaves of the butterbur supplemented the shade of the rampant willows, while a motionless grey stork stood sentry, watching for any frogs which had escaped the predations of the grass snakes.

All of this had for long years been overlooked by the mill, a broken-down square wooden slatted building with the huge paddle taking up most of the outer wall. The sense of dereliction was distressing, with most of the vanes of the paddle being broken and the paddle itself overwhelmed by climbing vegetation, a very public humiliation to ancient dignity. The roof had fallen in and the windows were empty eyes gazing sadly out over the river, mourning their lost past. The indifferent water meandered past with no salute to history; no respect for a partnership which had gone back centuries.

Eventually we arrived at the encampment. The contrast to the gypsy site was striking. We pushed past rubbish and piles of wooden slats until we got into the centre and found Fonso and Esmeralda waiting for us. Word had spread that we were coming.

'Florika, get the tea' called Esmeralda, bustling around to make sure we were comfortable. We all sat in plastic chairs under the striped awning, which, attached to the side of the caravan, created a passable room.

'Where's Trixie?' asked Florika as she passed around mugs of steaming tea.

'Still at home, but you'll see her in school again. She says you are really helping her.' Florika looked pleased at that.

'You've come about the strange things that have been happening' said Esmeralda. She was looking at Vadoma, and I could see that she sensed an empathy. Soon there were about twenty of the community about us, all watching and listening. They were talking among themselves in a strange dialect, but not threatening. Perhaps a kinship with Vadoma helped to abate their traditional suspicion of outsiders.

'We've been expecting something like this' Fonso said, suddenly looking very serious. 'The village is a place where a great many ley lines converge. They are passages of energy running through the earth which connect ancient pagan sites. They are a roadway for mystical activity and the church, the manor and the barn are right in the middle of them. These apparitions, these spiritual sensations, need energy to manifest themselves. They get it from two sources; the ley lines firstly, but in addition they need energy from a sympathetic person. This is why sightings are infrequent. They need a human input which only special people can provide.'

Vadoma nodded her head. It seemed everything was making sense to her, at least. The vicar and I looked at each other sceptically.

'We've heard reports of revenants being seen. Ask Charlie over there' said Fonso, pointing at a dwarf-like man who, suddenly finding himself the centre of attention, looked at the ground and shuffled behind some of his larger relatives.

'Revenants?' I asked. I was having real difficulty understanding what I was hearing. Mr Bollow was strangely quiet.

'Revenants are people who have returned from the dead, usually after a very long absence' Steve said. You could see his sudden comprehension about the strangers in the pub. 'But why now?'

'Well these things are usually triggered by the presence of a kindred spirit. A witch, for want of a better term.'

Looking at me, Esmeralda added 'And your family are the only newcomers?'

I looked at Vadoma. Her hands were covering her mouth, her eyes wide and staring.

'Granny!' we both said simultaneously.

CHAPTER SEVEN

As summer advanced, the garden, more of a wilderness than a garden, proved to be a wild and wonderful place for free-range children and other animals. The rampant growth was constantly threatening to overwhelm garages and broken-down old sheds and shamelessly devour anything left outside. Wind, rain and general decay contributed to the challenge of survival. The house alone seemed to hold its own, for the moment at least.

Every morning the tribe was kicked out to seek adventure, not to be expected back until the church bell struck one. This of course caused more argument, as most of the children, being a product of modern education, could neither count nor agree on the time (how could one come after twelve?), so the occasional tearful child would come in early to be patched up.

Down the centre of the wilderness a snaking path tried vainly to fight off the encroaching undergrowth, waiting to be overwhelmed by the green tide of the children's fantasy world. It was constantly witnessing battles between Al Capone (the good guys) and the contraband guys (the baddies). The path slunk darkly through the forest to the pond, where generations of mosquitoes, frogs and other monsters had been hatched. And then there was the graveyard just over the wall, which was normally left well alone after dark.

By autumn there had been several weeks of quiet normality and the village had settled down to its everyday lethargy. There had been no more unusual sightings, and we had not felt any more uncomfortable influences in the house. As Christmas was approaching, we felt confident enough to leave the house one dark and lonely night to see if Santa was making any early deliveries.

'Look carefully up at the sky, Ben, you might see Santa flying across the moon' I said. 'He has lots of deliveries to make at this time of the year.'

'Yeah right. Got a helicopter now, has he?' Well, at least my son is not easily led.

It was bitterly cold and the wind was whistling rudely through our holm oak, which in bloody-minded fashion always refused to shed its leaves in winter. The racing clouds produced a panorama of churning movement, with fearful shapes silhouetted against the deep blue of the night sky. Suddenly they slid back to expose an enormous moon. I heard a mournful howl from Rufus, quickly echoed in a different key by Muffin.

Then there came the sound of an enormous crash from the graveyard. The dogs immediately started barking like crazy. Ben, Trixie and Marianna all shouted at them to shut up because of the neighbours. We had to be very careful after the drama of the snails, a small episode but one which caused a disproportionate amount of anger. Mr Dodds had been complaining about how many there were when Ben helpfully suggested he should just throw them over the fence 'like my father does'. Mr Dodds has been rather cold to us ever since.

The side door to the vestry had blown open and someone appeared; the dark figure of the vicar. He was battling to try to force it closed and was pushing hard against the wind, the most unecclesiastical language surfing the gale towards us. Several pairs of eyes peered over the wall to witness the Lord's Representative battle against the forces of wind and darkness.

Then suddenly another clandestine figure loomed on to the scene, looking suspiciously like Mrs Dodds. Mrs Dodds and the vicar - meeting at midnight?

Vadoma, Marianna and I simultaneously exchanged knowing looks, while Trixie commented how nice it was that Mr Bollow was trying to save Mrs Dodds. Yet I saw an opportunity here to mend our relationship with Mr Dodds with this knowledge. It was well known that Mrs Dodds claimed to spend nights with her sister on a regular basis. I wondered what she was telling her husband.

The door was eventually closed and the vicar headed off towards the vicarage, while Mrs Dodds walked towards her sister's house. Creeping through the wild and unkempt graveyard, the children started howling like werewolves, with the dogs joining in. She picked up her skirts and fled, to be last seen vaulting the gate by the yew tree.

'Wow!' said Ben, 'We must ask Mr Dodds to put her forward for the Olympics.'

'No, don't mention this to him. I expect she wants it to be a surprise' said Marianna, choking back laughter. But her laughter died on her lips. Something had changed. The dogs knew it first. Suddenly we saw them stiffen and sink to the ground. Their hair had risen in spikes and the intensity of their eyes almost shone in the darkness. They crouched motionless, refusing to move. Rufus was emitting low, deep-throated growls.

'My god, look!' breathed Vadoma. The old church seemed now to show more sharply through the gloom. The faint light of the night sky had very subtly changed to a greenish hue, while the grass, the trees and the leaning and crooked headstones took on a white, salty harshness, as if a sudden frost had descended. And in the sky the night-clouds had seemed to stop to let the glow of the moon penetrate unhindered to the gravestones. Now there was a sudden, soundless invasion of acrobatic night-flyers… bats?, wheeling and dipping around the eaves of the church, a dark sea of fear made more horrific by their numbers. The wavering calls of owls sounded from the distant woods, while screeches and screams that surely could not have been uttered by any earthly animal echoed from the trees which had started to tremble and move in the breezeless, still air.

A low sulphurous mist then rose from the ground, condensing thickest over the oldest, the most sunken graves; the burnt smell of hell. Shapes and shadows floated from the trees towards the church and vanished into its structure.

Then, as if nothing had happened, the clouds continued their ageless journey, the gales of wind returned and the brimstone smell faded to memory. The chilly mantle which had enveloped us gave way to the sharp cold of a normal winter night.

'Come on, let's go inside' I said quietly, to try to bring sense back.

'All the noise must have woken the ancient sleepers' Vadoma said in hushed tones. Marianna's eyes looked unnaturally large and luminous in the whiteness of her face. The dogs, terrified, rushed back to the safety of their home. But the children seemed to be remarkably unruffled.

Back in the kitchen we found Granny, nose glowing red over a toothless smile.

'Why did we go outside?' asked Ben. 'Look, Rudolf's already here.' Obnoxious boy. But Granny did not seem to notice. She stamped crossly out of the kitchen for her retreat in the crow's-nest, but the cellar door was gently swinging on its hinges. We clearly had to see what mayhem Granny had left behind.

I climbed gingerly down the steps. The cavernous arches seemed part of an undersea grotto, dark, watery, covered in green fungus. But this place would have made a marine grotto look like a children's play area. Here cobwebs trailed and floated, invisible, detected only when their gentle, sticky kiss touched cheek or hand, waiting to snare the unprepared in the musty darkness.

I jumped at a sudden sound – a fizzing and then an abrupt pop as one of Granny's bottles of elderflower wine burst forth from its plastic bottle.

But those bottles filled with loving care by Granny now seemed cold and sinister in the subterranean darkness, their ends thrusting forth like the tentacles of an anemone to grip, tug and devour. Finding nothing unusual, I quickly rushed back towards the light, stubbing toes and jabbing fingers against rotten wood and slimy plaster. At last I was out of that subterranean hell. No wonder the children never go there.

But Granny loves it. She wants to live there and haunt it until the drink runs out. A ghastly thought – imagine a world haunted by drink-crazed grannies. Every cellar in the land stuffed with them, learning to reproduce, generating scores at a time like little jellyfish to waft maliciously through the air on a mission to colonise. No cellar, shop, pub or warehouse would be safe.

But there were no signs of breakages, no empty bottles hidden behind wooden cases, no cause for alarm. I closed the cellar door, noticing as I did so that the key had disappeared. And just at that moment there floated up the stairs, very indistinctly, what seemed to be a brief scraping of hob-nailed boots, and the sound of a large wooden object being dragged across the floor. Then silence.

I took a deep breath and went back down the stairs again, dreading to think what I might see. But no changes revealed themselves in the flickering light.

'I must get those lights fixed' I said to Alison, who was just hearing about the visions by the church.

'The vicar called earlier' she said in a worried voice. 'He wants to come around tomorrow with Fonso and Steve. He says more strange things have been happening.'

CHAPTER EIGHT

The next morning, over the usual chaotic breakfast, there was a sense of agitation around the room. Marianna looked awful. I could see dark rings under puffy eyes, hair lank, and she had made no effort at make-up. She was talking quietly to Granny.

'What's up?' I asked.

'I had a terrible dream. Granny's been telling me what it means.'

'Oh dear, sorry about that. Do you want to tell us about it?' I leaned over to pour her a cup of strong coffee, lightly placing my hand on her shoulder as a gesture of comfort. She leaned into me slightly. I did not respond; Alison was watching.

'I was chased by a shadow, a shape near the river. Then I got lost in these big, great weeds in a wasteland. There were tall plants growing above my head, hiding the sun, no light, no warmth. They were bending over to touch me and trying to bend their stalks around me to sting and hurt me and strangle me. Then the river suddenly went rushing past flooding all the land and I saw the plants moving and waving in the water trying to catch my legs. I got really frightened. Then a tsunami must have struck, because even more water in huge waves covered everywhere. I was being swamped and felt myself drowning, sinking, choking in the water. Then from out of the water I saw – a pair of eyes. Evil, horrible eyes. And there was a knife, a sharp knife coming towards me. Suddenly I felt a terrible pain, and then I woke up. I didn't know where I was, my head was hurting and I was sweating. My sheets were soaked and the room was very cold.'

'Ah yes' Granny said, in her element. 'That shadow that was chasing you tells me you haven't got over that bad experience in London when you were stalked by that man. You must try to get over it, and then the shadow will go. And the water is the passage of your life. This is you, Marianna. You're trying to control your emotions and to understand and accept what has happened. But the tsunami and the water burying you shows you haven't been able to cope with it all, you haven't handled the stress and events are overwhelming you, life is going too fast. And the drowning shows this fear. And all the plants show your spiritual difficulty with moving on. When it happens again you need to try to control everything, try to pull up or destroy the plants. In the water you need to keep relaxed and quiet, then all the floods will go calm. That's when you will have beaten your fears.

'But come up and see me later and we can talk about it some more. I'll give you a sleep potion. A mixture of aconite and arnica will help. But we have to be very careful! Aconite is wolfsbane, and that's very poisonous. They used to tip their arrows with it many hundreds of years ago. Let's ask Steve about it. There might be records of it being used on the bodies in the graveyard!'

'OK Marianna, that's you sorted' I said sarcastically. Marianna looked unconvinced and left to go to her room, but Vadoma was nodding enthusiastically in agreement. 'I come to help too' she said to Granny.

'But that's not all' Granny added quietly, looking to see that Marianna was out of earshot. 'I sensed a problem coming in the future; but I don't know what it will be.'

'Now listen everybody' I moved on. 'The vicar, Fonso, Steve and Gavin will be coming here about elevenish. They want to talk to us about what happened at the church last night.'

'Mrs Dodds might be able to help' suggested Ben. He didn't understand why this comment brought him a frosty look from Vadoma.

'No, he wants to talk to us about other things as well' said Alison. 'There have been more strange things happening in the village.'

'Granny will be here too, so Ben, you MUST behave' I told him. Ben had recently got a real bee in his bonnet about Granny needing help; she had to banish those illusions about youth. He had been told that she had once been a young girl called Petronella, but this seemed unlikely. To him, the old had always lived in the same world of pressed flowers, drawers of ancient spread-eagled butterflies, cases of stuffed birds keeping watch through unblinking glass eyes. Children could not see the youth inside the prune-like body.

The news that the vicar was dropping by the next day

prompted Ben to open a book about the reason for the visit, as Granny had trained him to do. It read:

1/ leer at Marianna and Vadoma

2/ Leer at Alison

3/ Exciting times with Muffin

4/ Family pastoral care

The first two were pretty even odds.

Around noon they all eventually arrived. Upon smelling the fresh baking from the kitchen, they sidled in with happy anticipation through the back door. Muffin was ecstatic at a visit from her black labrador, but Rufus gave him a glare that said 'You put a foot wrong and I'll have you'. With much ducking of heads everybody managed to avoid the flypapers and grabbed handfuls of warm scones and dripping butter on their way through to the kitchen.

'What happy children!' said the vicar.

'Good morning vicar, a coffee to wash your scone down?' asked Lyn.

'And the currants' innocently added Trixie.

They filed into the drawing room with Lyn balancing coffees on a plastic tray, cups sliding around, to meet Mrs Knight, who was already ensconced with Marianna. There was great relief on Mrs Knight's face when she saw Ben wasn't there; he could not resist staring at her pregnancy bump and making innocent but inappropriate comments.

Alison had recently told him to stop eating so many sweets or he'd get fat, so he earnestly told Mrs Knight 'I know what you've been doing'. This made her blush uncontrollably. To further her discomfort she then saw Rufus standing in the corner staring at her with unbridled interest, tongue lolling, with a pink telescope protruding impertinently out of his underfur.

The vicar chose this moment to launch into an obscure diatribe about immorality, clearly directed at our household. Apparently the good Mrs Dodds had been complaining that every so often she could hear shouts of 'Take your clothes off' from several members of the household, including Marianna. As a highly moral lady and stalwart of the church, she had asked the vicar to look into this disgraceful behaviour.

Marianna laughed out loud, to the vicar's great indignation.

'Rufus goes for walkies in his coat' she explained. The dog got to his feet with an expectant yap. 'Oh dear, he heard that - no Rufus, not now! When we get back we always say 'Take your clothes off' to him. That's all it is!

'Ah. Oh, I see. Of course, I knew there would be an innocent explanation' said the vicar. 'Mrs Dodds will be so relieved.' I thought he looked slightly disappointed.

And so back to the point of our meeting.

Gavin began 'Yes, it all seems to be starting again. I was walking past the old barn a few nights ago at about midnight when I heard voices. I sneaked quietly up to the far wall where there are vent holes and peeked in. I still can't believe what I saw, it was like a medieval pageant. There seemed to be a meeting going on. A woman was led into the centre of the room by two big blokes, men dressed in dark leather coats and white shirts. They had black breeches on and thigh boots and broad-brimmed hats. Around the room there must have been scores of other men, all dressed about the same.

'The woman didn't look too good. Her hair was matted and filthy. She was wearing a coarse woollen dress and her skin was spotted with dirt and disease. She looked as if she was ridden with lice and fleas. I could see raw scratch marks, all red and swollen. Someone shouted 'Tie her hands together so she doesn't fly away'. There was a jeering crowd of onlookers crushed against the side and back walls, all dressed in dark colours.

'The woman was pushed on to the chair in the middle of the space, facing a long table behind which were five men, all dressed like priests. The man in the centre stood up, and then the whole scene disappeared. There was complete silence and the barn was back to normal.'

'I have heard of these things too' said Fonso, his normally hostile face suddenly transformed into one of deep understanding. 'Sometimes a time slip occurs, a time portal opens up when there is a particular moment on the ley lines and it's possible to see back into history, just for a moment.' He turned to me. 'This must have happened near the time when you saw the apparitions going into the church. Something close to the village pulled the trigger. Gavin, what you saw must have been the trial of a witch.'

'That's what I wondered' said Steve. 'The old barn was a place of judgement and execution about four hundred years ago. So what have you seen, Fonso?'

'You know the old mill?' continued Fonso. 'I was there one

81

cold, blustery night when the moon was very bright. As I watched, the wheel started turning, all covered with green and brown water plants. Among the weeds we saw a body, entangled and rotating with the wheel, emerging with a loud sucking noise until it was submerged again. It kept going round and round. When I looked closer I saw that it was the decomposed body of a man. The water was boiling with movement, from strange things I could not see. And then it rapidly passed as the clouds distorted the light. Everything faded. The next day we went there to look, but the wheel was just as we had seen it before. It certainly hadn't moved during the night, it couldn't have. The cogs and machinery were still rusted blocks. The wooden wheel was still broken spokes and anchored in the mud.'

The vicar looked deeply uncomfortable. Nothing in his ecclesiastical training had prepared him for this.

'We all know that spirits live with God, but the living cannot, do not, have access to the afterlife' he said. 'We cannot cross that threshold.'

Eventually I took my leave to look more closely at the barn. The vicar got back on to his bike for his next meeting at the Green Man. He wobbled off with that irritating 'I'm saving the planet' smugness. We often wondered how he missed the traffic. Maybe those heading towards him get out of his way, while he sees simultaneously those coming from left and right.

We all looked at each other in frozen consternation. What we had experienced in our house was mild compared to this.

CHAPTER EIGHT

Were the sounds from the cellar, the sudden changes in temperature, a ghostly premonition of worse to come?

And then the screeching of tyres came from outside the house.

'Come quickly, it's Granny!' a voice shouted hysterically.

CHAPTER NINE

I felt a huge impact and instantly began to float away. I looked down and found I was lying in the road. I glanced along my body and saw my clothes torn, my arms and legs bloodied and contorted. A deep and searing agony through every part of my flesh made my head spin. I was swimming in pain.

I was floating in and out of my body, hovering on the borders of earthly death. All around me was chaos, noise and panic. And then somebody picked me up. I didn't see who it was as sounds, colours and pain were mingling in an overwhelming blur of sensation. They were speaking to me, but I knew not what they were saying.

As I drifted away again I saw clearly all my young family around me, Alison trying to make me comfortable, Vadoma and Marianna shouting for help, the children being led away by their father back into the house. And strangers watching, talking quietly. A car against the wall, its front dented and stained with blood. My blood?

And then the ambulance arrived and they moved me in and took me away. I had gone again, but followed out of curiosity and sadness. The lights and noise of the vehicle produced a wondrous contrast and gave me a new sense of peace, the tranquillity of certainty. Then I was going down a long white passage into a sparse bedroom, where I suddenly felt a hand on my forehead and heard a calm but desperate voice pleading with me to respond.

As I drifted back, the world I was watching disappeared and I was in that warm comfortable bed, with my body being examined and tubes and wires attached. But I was no longer a spectator. Someone closed my eyes and then mercifully I began to drift and float again. I found myself looking down upon my collections of plants in my sanctuary in the attic. My old chair was so welcoming. But suddenly gentle ocean waves appeared, and started to caress me and carry me along a watery tunnel of translucent light, not to suffocation or drowning but to comfort and security. I tried to move my tongue, but no words would come out.

'Mum, please stay with us!' Alison was pleading. Now the watchers were being taken out of my room. I lay there a long time, hovering on the edge. After a while I started rising again, but this time it was different. I was being pulled; no gentle hands now but a harsh tugging. I looked down and saw myself as once I was; slim, a halo of fair hair around a finely-balanced face, elegant and artistic fingers resting either side of my slender body, almost boyish with long tapering legs. I was beautiful, once. And there were my small breasts. I smiled at their memory. They had taken so long to appear, and were such a disappointment, to me at least. The rampant hair between my legs which needed constant attention…

This young girl, the young girl I was, was the cause of the weeping and the frenzied activity. I was proud! I knew now that people cared. But the battery of machines, wires and pipes attached to that beautiful young body seemed a violation. I understood not the commotion, the weeping, except for my lovely Vadoma, who was in the corner, reaching out to me.

She was sitting on a hard white plastic chair, her brow furrowed in concentration. Her body was tense and her eyes were closed. I knew her mind was ranging widely over her world, building images of the time we had spent together, a deeply focused effort to tune into my mind. I watched as her breathing got shallower and faster, her fingers and hands clenched in her lap in a semi-trance as she fought to bridge the gap between our worlds. Then, as she got closer to my world, her head dropped forward, her body became agitated and she started mumbling, her shoulders twitching. A pallor spread over her skin.

And then we met. Her face, drawn so tight, now relaxed and was still. Her breathing became normal, as if she was sleeping.

'*Babushka, Babushka, please come home!*' she wordlessly begged. I smiled at her, filled with gentleness and love. I must travel, I told her. I had friends to meet again, a chance to leave the loneliness of my old age. She could come with me, if she was able. So she intensified her efforts to keep with me. I felt almost a physical joining as I started to move away. As I looked back I saw her slumped in her chair, her eyes closed, Alison trying to revive her too. Dear Alison, there was just too much to understand, too much commotion. Her soft, gentle desperation, her tears, her anguish and distress as strangers hooked me up to all the tubes and wires. But still the forces pulled me deeper into that dark tunnel of moving waves. I was enveloped and tossed around, all the while moving irrevocably away from my body. I realised that I was not alone; other souls were moving with me, many in extreme distress, screaming soundlessly, eyes wide and unblinking in terror, especially the younger ones who had had no time to prepare for the end of their earthly lives.

Then the tunnel dissolved and I stood on the pristine edge of a brilliant world.

'I've arrived' I said to Vadoma. She did not answer, but I felt her presence.

It was a world I knew well from my youth, my previous existence. It was an inspiring mix of times, people and history. Far away, over hills of sharply defined green, down a glittering path meandering through flowers and trees of wondrous shape and colour, a mystical city appeared. It seemed to hover above anchored reality, high and clear against a horizon of the brightest blue. Although a stranger, I recognised everything but the colours and smells wafting over me were new. It seemed like a symbolic world where only the best emotions could exist.

I walked in awe towards the city, my bare feet moving effortlessly down the path towards my final destiny. The flowers, the trees, the balmy breeze blended into a harmony of musical energy which drew me on. And now Vadoma, my wonderful gypsy friend, was with me. As I walked, all my faults, all my disappointments, my failures, were embraced and dismissed. I began to see all the little strings of casual events in my life, how a careless word, an unthinking action had caused wounds which rippled outwards to hurt and maim. Worse, my acts of kindness had been few. I was ashamed of myself, and humbled that Vadoma could see my penitence.

It was then that I began to see my life stretching back into the distance down the centuries. As I walked my heart leapt; I could see my beloved Bertie coming towards me. My heart stopped at the sight of his handsome, smiling face as he welcomed me. His uniform was as usual immaculate; he was dressed to fight, and of course to die and leave me a widow.

My parents were there, both looking exactly as they had always looked. My father was dressed in a grey suit and I saw again the familiar broken nose, the short cropped hair and grey moustache. On his weather-beaten face was a good-humoured welcome. My mother was dressed as usual in a casual, loose-fitting skirt and blouse for the day's gardening. I cried and ran towards them, but to my surprise and distress, they faded away.

I walked on, and as I moved back in time the wonderful softness began to change to a harsher reality, a world where life had less value, where mercy was not a human gift but a weakness. I could hear Vadoma whispering in my ear *'Come back! Come back! It is not what you expect.'*

But I kept on, driven by a remorseless curiosity to see my

beginnings, to understand the start of existence. I passed through the carnage of two great wars. Then I stopped, rooted to the spot. Here was Bertie again, on the battlefield. He was not smiling now. He was leading a charge, shouting, furiously running, urging his men on.

And then he was cut down in a bleak effort to push forwards; a forlorn exercise in following orders. I felt his agony, his anguish and panic, his last moments of remorse and misery as he knew he would never be going home. I saw his fleeting sadness at losing me, his parents and his family. 'Why, why, why?' he was soundlessly asking before oblivion mercifully descended. But not before his keening wail burst forth in a primeval howl of grief. The grief of his unselfish loss and the helpless anger that so much should be taken by those who ordered the destruction, but did not share the horror and the danger.

Now as I walked on towards the city in the sky, it began to lose its lustre. The shining glass and steel structure seemed to be sinking. The buildings became dull, dark wood and unfinished stone, small windows, dark shadows. A sense of overhanging fear began to make itself felt.

As I moved back in time I also saw momentarily the wonders of science and social mobility. I saw the movement to freedom, the march of liberation. To be briefly a part of that, to witness the bravery and courage behind it, was truly humbling. To see the social upheaval decades before, when Darwin published his evolution and social theories, to see how the traditional views of religion were mocked, was an inspiration for truth and courage. I could feel Vadoma, who was still travelling with me, expanding her consciousness, but still trying to persuade me to come back. 'I must travel this path Vadoma, we move together' I told her.

Then I passed a humble cottage. Inside it in a small room, a middle-aged man with long, wiry grey hair and a full beard and moustache was writing at his desk by the light of the window. His eyes looked up and momentarily held mine with an expression of great depth and understanding, an academic treatise open before him as he worked to translate his vision into words. I knew who he was; Karl Marx, fifty years before left-wing intellectuals would embrace his communist ideals. To be in his presence was a fulfilment in itself, to pay homage to such an immense figure of the nineteenth century was a deep honour. But then he too faded and was gone.

And so I moved past all types of wonders... but now I had to stop, linger and watch. Here was a clean-shaven man with bushy white sideburns and fiercely-arched eyebrows who was staring down a primitive microscope and taking notes. I realised he was studying infection and disease and that his studies would one day lead to a whole new approach to medicine and surgery. Joseph Lister had always been my inspiration when I was studying natural medicine in my youth. Vadoma too was in awe of these early intellectual giants.

'Why can I not speak to them?' I asked her. I could see she was still hunched in her white chair in my hospital room.

'Because your time has not yet come' she answered.

And then history passed me in an accelerating blur as I leapt the centuries. There were glimpses of warfare in Europe, in Asia, in Arabia; opium wars in China; expansion into Africa, the opening up of North and South America; the Crimea, which inspired modern nursing. I saw the harsh conditions which powered the Industrial Revolution, the awful housing, the huge families who worked all hours, young children too, and still couldn't feed themselves. But it was all passing in a rush so fast that comprehension was impossible. I longed to stop and savour the reality, but it was hopeless.

Until suddenly my travels slowed and I found myself in another battlefield. I felt myself pulled back as if at the end of a rope. Everywhere I looked I saw fires burning, on the distant hills and closer, as wooden carts, piles of clothing and bodies blazed.

I felt myself there, trapped in the scene and unable to move on. Throat-catching acrid smoke drifted everywhere. My vision was blurred and the sharp, stinging air burnt my eyes and drew tears. Buildings collapsed. There was debris ankle deep, armour, body parts, dead people, mutilated animals. Bright banners rippled in the wind as hordes of blood-splashed men moved across the blackened, scorched landscape. I heard the noise of the battle, the explosions, the screams from horribly-wounded soldiers, the terror of the horses. I shared the fear of young men who had left their homes on a great adventure, only to find the bleak and brutal reality of pain and sorrow.

Remorselessly this scene of horror continued to unfold in slow motion. My senses were overwhelmed, but I could not look away, nor could I continue my journey. I saw little bands of gaudily-dressed men, defeated and bloodied, being rounded up by brown-suited, sober-looking soldiers on horseback. They all shuffled away towards what must have been the prison, an area of large tents, policed by groups of men with an air of command amid the desolate landscape.

And then suddenly, to my horror, I found I was no longer a spectator. I had become the centre of attention. I saw the grinning face of a big, lanky soldier looking at me. He snapped his fingers and a group of rough-hewn men grabbed me and threw me on to the back of a cart, already loaded with other women, all wailing with sorrow and suffering. They were guilty of nothing more than searching among the bodies for their loved ones, but this was enough for arrest and interrogation.

After a short ride in the cart we were unloaded and pushed wordlessly into a cold stone-walled room and the door slammed and bolted. There must have been a dozen of us crammed into this darkness and we could not even lie down. There was nothing in the room but a single stinking bucket. The cold was intense.

'*Babushka, your time has not yet come*' once again echoed in my mind. Vadoma was still passing strength and courage to me.

After timeless hours and days the door was unbolted and light flooded in again. I was dragged out and taken by the soldiers into a large barn. By now I was filthy – my hair was matted and my clothes were stiff with grime and dirt. My skin itched and was covered in sores from lice and biting insects.

There was a solitary chair in the middle of the barn, which

leaned unsteadily on the uneven dirt floor. A row of five smartly-dressed priests faced the chair from behind a long oak table upon which lay manuscripts and books. Around the sides of the barn was a large gathering of local people, obviously there to watch and to jeer. They were all dressed in sober puritanical clothes. Many clutched bibles and religious texts. Their pious, manic devotion gave a frightening gravity to my situation.

As I shuffled to the chair one of the women shouted 'tie her hands together so she doesn't fly away!' and my heart stopped. I now understood that I was being accused of witchcraft.

The priest in the centre of the table, who was obviously the judge, now rose. In a kindly, gentle voice he told me that I was being tried for witchcraft; he urged me to repent. Many witnesses had seen me scorning God and worshipping Satan. My spells and potions were well known within the community.

'I try to cure people of their illnesses! I try to help people!' I whispered in desperation. But the judge, suddenly no longer kindly, spoke sharply. 'Do not interrupt!' he snapped. 'You condemn yourself by distorting God's will through trying to delay the passage of those he has called. And by defending heresy you commit heresy.'

There then followed a long stream of witnesses. I was blamed for the untimely death of a baby girl belonging to a family called Watkins. There had been a period of many months when no births had happened in the village, because I had cursed it with sterility. The summer crops had been largely destroyed by drought the previous year, and some hayricks had caught fire spontaneously during the heat of that summer. Satan had been seen late at night dancing on a cross by my house. The litany went on and on. I had given sanctuary to a large number of 'familiars', including toads, dogs and cats, who lived in or close to my house.

Then, at a command, my guards leapt upon me and tore away my shirt. They sought the extra nipple, the 'witch's mark', from which my animals, or Satan, would suckle. My humiliation was complete. The crowd surged forwards to witness my nakedness and shame, and I saw the lust in the eyes of the judges and the male onlookers whose hypocrisy and enjoyment in my nudity was shameful. The judges ordered me to stand and I was stripped completely. They then examined me more closely to find the mark. My body was covered in sores and any mark would have done for their purpose, but they still took many minutes looking at me intimately before finding me guilty. Then I was ordered to cover my immodesty and accused of publicly displaying myself, because I had not admitted my crime to avoid having to do so.

I was now dragged away through the onlookers, who surged forward to get a closer look. The remains of self-respect were banished by their cries. 'Devil's Spawn!' they shouted. 'Satan!' 'Kill her now!'

The abuse was endless. As they tried to hit me and kick me, I heard again '*Babushka, your time is not yet, come home now!*' And at last I followed that instruction. The meeting of our two minds transcended the centuries and now, willingly enough, I let myself be hauled back. I saw the room where my body was lying. Around it a new clamour had begun. Vadoma was on her feet guarding my body and insisting with great passion 'She is coming back! I feel her, I see her, she is coming back!' White-clad people were trying to get to my bedside. And Alison, looking at Vadoma and sensing the truth and urgency, was responding to the confusion and disorder by shouting 'No! We've changed our minds, we will not turn it off.'

Instantly there was quiet. The new instruction had to be assimilated, to be discussed.

At last I returned to my body. I was once again an old woman with aches and pains. My deafness and bad eyesight were almost a comfort when I recalled the other side. 'I won't die now' I whispered. 'My time is not yet come.' I looked around for Vadoma and there she was, tears streaming down her face. Alison, clearly in shock and trembling, was holding my hands as I closed my eyes, this time to sleep.

Alison hugged Vadoma and the nurses quietly left the room. They had witnessed a miracle.

'Look at those bite marks, those red lumps and swellings!' said Alison. 'Oh Mum, what's been happening to you?'

Vadoma shrugged her shoulders in a pretence of ignorance. But the secret was in her eyes.

CHAPTER TEN

With Granny's recovery came the spring. Suddenly the first warmth was kissing the garden with the gradual awakening of green in every tree, and the bright colours of early bulbs were bringing a festive look to the wet, dank brownness. The pond in the forest was no longer a frozen mirror to flatter the distant midnight moon as it glided gently through the harsh winter coldness. The owls would no longer whisper-wing quietly and menacingly over the frozen rustlings and icy surfaces. The icicles, their translucent teardrops mourning the loss of their beauty, dripped off the trees like inverted crystal cathedral spires, while the winter mist which had nightly swathed the buildings and the stones in the churchyard with a clammy whiteness was suddenly less dense, less intimidating.

Gradually the warm breath of spring caressed away the winter blues. Spring would bring tree climbing and the joys of hiding in the top of the laurel bushes to pull faces at Mr Dodds over the wall; and the fun of chucking clods of earth causing irritation and commotion to his dogs. The murmuring, clicking and whispering of newborn life had begun, bringing insects, tadpoles and frogs to set Ben on yet another collision course with his family and neighbours. He could once again put jars of tadpoles in the larder to be discovered by Lynn, making the excuse that they needed to be close to the food, so they knew they wouldn't starve. Lynn would walk in rigid disgust out to the pond to let them go. Ben, the budding scientist, wanted to attach a microchip to their tails to discover where they slept, until Marianna uncharitably pointed out that their tails disappear as they get older. More disillusion for Ben, and a further topic of magic and dark forces to discuss with the Vicar. Rufus and Muffin don't lose their tails, so tadpoles must be under some woeful influence from the graveyard? Perhaps the Vicar would like to stay up one night to watch the pond with him? The Bishop then might pay him more money and he 'wouldn't have to ask us to put our button collections and foreign coins into the Sunday shakedown'.

And then there was the mud. Rainwater and old soggy leaves from the winter were once again being trodden into the house as outdoor excursions became more frequent and longer. 'Take off your boots in the kitchen!' played over and over as if on a tape loop. There was a daily smell of wet dog, spiced by the occasional dead squirrel brought in triumph to Sunday lunch for the family to enjoy and left disjointed on the kitchen tiles with Marianna and Lynn yelling in unison 'get it out!' But there would be nobody left to obey, for animals and children had cascaded back to the garden to look for more delicacies.

As the ice melted we would no doubt witness the flooding of the septic tank with the downhill seepage to Mr Dodds' vegetable patch. He would never agree with our argument that this was a neighbourly service to save him having to buy expensive fertiliser. Certainly his cabbages, brussels sprouts and spinach were the envy of the horticultural society, although it was lucky the judges did not taste them before awarding the rosettes in the summer show. He was regularly accused of cheating, but Mrs Dodds would insist that the vicar should do his Christian duty and support the oppressed. The arguments could get very heated and personal, but Mrs Dodds was deemed to be charitable in her support for the vicar, who inevitably had to call another meeting in the Green Man. These meetings usually either ended in a free for all, or everyone parted the best of friends. Unfortunately nobody, least of all the vicar, could remember the next day what had been decided. This made another meeting necessary. So went the rural cycle, with seasons, customs and the minutes of parish council meetings eternally repeating themselves.

But an evil influence had started to infiltrate the Horticultural Society, one which threatened its very survival; the 'furreners' from the North and Midlands who spoke with strange accents and had even stranger customs. They had started to buy second homes in the village. Worse, they had the temerity not only to enter the competitions but sometimes to win them. It was clear that they must be bringing 'furren tricks' with them, so a petition was organised to ask Tesco, Sainsbury and Waitrose to close their vegetable departments within a fifty-mile radius of the village during the competition to stop such skulduggery. But it was a constant mystery, and the cause of much discussion - whatever had happened to the petition letters, because none of the departments was ever closed.

Then Perce, a sharp-eyed gaffer of poor health but excellent eyesight, noticed that Darrell the Postman was driving a new Mondeo. This news had to be treated with caution, because Darrell was a mountain of a man with an evil expression and equally vile breath, usually exhaled through a thicket of beard, gravy and Cornish pasty crumbs. Those who got too close were showered with food fragments, often several days old. Darrell was always grinning evilly, his yellow and black teeth bared like an old bulldog's. He seemed to have been spending a suspicious amount of time in the Dodds' submerged vegetable patch... but who was going to be the accuser?

On the surface village life continued as normal, following a centuries-old pattern of seasonal change, births, marriages and deaths, of social rivalry, fumbling infidelity and petty crime. A timeless routine, yet Alison and I were among those who did not trust the peace and the comforting predictability to last. It was as if the strange happenings of a few months ago were sleeping, waiting, gathering strength for a new and more serious onslaught; one which would arrive without warning.

One morning in the Green Man I broached the subject with Steve.

'Have you felt anything lately – you know, anything odd?' I asked him.

99

'It's not all over, if that's what you mean.' He gave me a sly look.

'I can feel something awakening' I said. The village is changing. There's a sense of tension. I get it at home in the Manor and I feel it around the church. What do you think?' Marianna was gazing at Steve. She was getting hooked by all this spooky stuff, and he knew it.

'You're right' he said. 'You have to start by understanding the history of the village - the ley lines, the paganism, the conflict between the various belief systems, the sheer scale of murder, execution and random killing the village has seen over thousands of years. It's all centred on the Manor and the church, because that's where it all happened. But you have to know how to see it.'

'Can you teach us?' said Marianna, her eyes glowing.

'If you like I'll take you around the church and we can examine the carvings, the pictures and the stone working. That will give you some insight into the beliefs and truths of previous generations. It's been lost in modern living, but it's there below the surface, waiting for release. We can go to the cellars and the catacombs, you'll get a real sense of the mystery, the horrors of the other worlds. A lot of this history is in the church - you'll see for yourself.'

'OK, but you're not taking the children' said Alison. 'They can go to friends. Ben can go to the Forge and Trixie can spend the day with Florika.'

And so it was decided that Marianna and Steve would visit

the church the next day. Vadoma would take Trixie to Florika and Ben would be dropped off with the blacksmith. Everyone would have such an interesting day.

If only we had known what was around the corner.

CHAPTER ELEVEN

It was a brash, windy morning when Steve and Marianna stood by the lych gate. The wind was tossing leaves around in twists and spirals and the brown, papery shapes chased each other in butterfly swirls, a final dance of death before decay and decomposition took hold. From there new life would spring; the eternal circle.

'Sure you're ready for this?' asked Steve.

'I can't wait!' answered Marianna, but something made her shiver and draw her thin coat more tightly around her slim figure; whether it was the cold, a wariness of what was to come or simply Steve's wandering eyes, she could not be sure.

'Before we go in, we need to understand some history' Steve began, getting into lecturing mode. 'How religion and the church graduated from the early days of magic into specific beliefs and eventually, some people think, will end in science. Around and inside this church we can see magic and religious belief merging and developing over several thousand years. In ancient Celtic times this village was a religious sanctuary which had close connections with other religious spots. That's why we believe the ley lines concentrate here and build really strong energy influences. But this psychic activity, or what we would call paranormal afterlife, was to the ancients the norm. They had no concept of heaven and hell. There were no rewards or punishment for their behaviour in earthly life and a continuation to the afterlife was automatic.

'They also had many gods, who were unpredictable and had to be soothed and flattered by their priests, the Druids. So there was constant movement between religious areas and where these paths crossed, these ley lines resulted in strong beliefs and influences which we no longer really understand today.'

'I know. I hear about these things but proof seems to be impossible' said Marianna.

'Yes. But let's look first at the surrounding countryside, and the animals. The ancients worshipped the sun and many animals and features of nature, such as the sinister, darkly hooded ravens, mountains and forest glades. Certain trees, like the oak, were of huge significance. They also worshipped springs and some stretches of water. Many of their gods could adopt animal shapes and disguises, and there was no clear distinction between life and death, so their magic was everywhere.

'In fact in early November when the end of summer passes into winter there was a festival where the living could visit the dead. So early religion was all about nature. Human shapes didn't come into it until much later, when the Romans came to Britain. They brought gods in human shape with them. It was remarkable that the ancients were so flexible, because they seem to have accepted new gods alongside the old, though it took many centuries for the old beliefs to be replaced entirely. Of course this is when Christianity started to take hold - the amazing replacement of all those individual and community gods with just the one.'

'This is the same in my country. We have many gods, but we have vampires too. You know about Count Dracula?' Marianna was really getting into the spirit of it all.

'Of course, he's very well known in Western Europe too, he's starred in enough films! But let's walk around the church and you can see the Norman structure.' He took her arm and she allowed herself to be led forward.

'The church was built on top of several layers of prehistoric sanctuaries which we know about. Six ritual shafts were discovered about a hundred years ago. In pagan times they allowed communication with the underworld, and they were filled with sacrificial offerings, usually of flesh which could be human, and animal bones. They would also throw wooden figures and phallic carvings into them. You will see more when we go into the catacombs.'

Marianna shivered. A feeling of cold crept over her body, yet curiosity still overcame her doubts. There was something intriguing about Steve, in spite of an obvious interest in her which was far from intellectual. And an uncomfortable sense of premonition she felt deep inside.

'During the excavations they found a corner of a ditched enclosure' Steve went on. 'The rest is under the church. This is where the ritual pits were discovered. There were sacrificial stacks of human and animal bones, piles of iron swords and knives which had been offered to the gods with the bodies of men and women. There had been wholesale decapitations, and bodies had been ritually dismembered and stripped of their flesh.' He looked at her, testing her reaction. Marianna shuddered.

'Sorry, not nice is it! You OK?'

'Yes yes, I want to know.'

'The bones and skulls were then carefully stacked and stored. What gave added significance to the sanctuary was the closeness of the river. Even today the occasional skeleton is discovered, because there were sacrifices to the water spirits. These human sacrifices really upset the Romans, but in reality they just wanted an excuse to rid the land of the Druids. The Druids were a non-tribal group who could travel freely without danger, so they were a constant threat to the Romans, because they were a force which could unite the tribes.'

'This is so like our history' murmured Marianna.

'And then after the Romans left there were wide movements of tribes across Europe. You've heard of King Arthur, I'm sure. He was at the forefront in resisting invasions from Europe. This was the Dark Ages. We don't know very much about that time because there was so little written history, although we've found evidence of wonderful metalwork and illuminated manuscripts in the religious centres, especially in Ireland. You know the story of King Arthur throwing his sword into the lake when he was dying?'

'I have seen the film. We like Monty Python in Rumania.'

'Ha! Well yes... but it's a wonderful legend. It was an echo from prehistory when they used to sacrifice swords and knives to the gods, especially the water gods. This is why we find them in burial sites and ritual shafts. But anyway I can ramble on forever about this. Are you sure I'm not boring you?' He gave her a piercing smile.

'No, this really is interesting. Let's walk now around the churchyard.'

'Of course.' He led the way between the rows of tumbledown graves.

'Now, most of these graves go back hundreds of years, but all we can see now is the stones. The lettering has been worn away by the wind and rain. So we have to guess who they were and how they died. But there are some more recent records which I can show you.'

As they moved through the gate and into the graveyard, Marianna again felt that cold, brittle trembling which seemed to dig even deeper into her. But she could hardly pull out now.

There was a wide gravel path up to the church door, which split into two and then snaked around the church to form a circle. They took the path to the left, where most of the graves were relatively recent. There were still flowers on some of them, and even a bedraggled teddy bear sat by what must have been a child's resting place. But in the spring sunshine there was no hint of any fear, terror or inexplicable forces, just a restful feeling of peace, a quietness and solitude. But still Marianna felt uncomfortable. As they continued around the church they came to rows of older gravestones, many leaning over and sinking into the soft earth as if mourning the fact that earthly life should so quickly be neglected and forgotten.

Between the graves the bright spring grass was starting its annual journey of growth, with crocuses and primroses paying a colourful tribute to the solemnity and pathos of mostly bleak lives which had ended with few mourning their passage. As they walked further Marianna noticed a forlorn, deserted corner bordered by a stone wall with yew trees separating one patch, overgrown with brambles and nettles, from the rest of the yard. There were no gravestones or memorials here of any sort, and she knew immediately that it was from here the sense of menace emanated.

Marianna shuddered. 'What is that place?' she whispered.

'It's an area of unconsecrated ground where the murderers and the worst of the executed criminals were buried. There's no written record of these people, so we have to rely on word of mouth for their stories. Animals avoid the place, even today.'

As they hurried past Marianna looked over her shoulder as if half-expecting to see a spectre rising from the ground to follow them, but there was nothing. Then, as they turned the corner and the rest of the churchyard came into view, the air seemed to lighten. Finally they found themselves back at the main door.

'Everywhere you look around the outside of this building you see the Norman style' said Steve. 'We'll see signs of the pagan times when we go to the catacombs which were built by digging through the old sites. There are many tales about hauntings and mysterious deaths when the ancient bones were disturbed, but thankfully it was all hundreds of years ago. See that arched entrance, how solid and massive it is? And at the far end is the square tower - typical Norman architecture. Now, look up there at those narrow long windows, with the pointed shapes. They were added about two hundred years later. There was a great fire which burned down the roof. Inside you'll see the old barrel-shaped ceiling has virtually disappeared and has been replaced by a flatter fan-vaulted structure. It's quite spectacular.

'There were many rumours documented at the time that the fire was started deliberately - punishment for disturbing the sacred pagan relics. It was even suggested that there had been a mass rising from the graves to seek retribution. The woman who claimed to see it was hanged as a witch. In fact she might even be buried in that patch of unconsecrated ground. See those hideous faces on those stone outcrops at the corners? Gargoyles! Lovely, aren't they? They were put in all these old churches to take rain away from the walls, but the stonemasons had some fun with them. Rumour has it that the faces were medieval cartoons of dignitaries, just to tease them, to make them see how ugly and grotesque the greed of public office had made them. The word gargoyle is related to gargle, you know. It refers to the throat, comes from a French verb, *gargouiller.*'

'When I hear Granny gargling her mixtures next time I'll tell her to come to the church and she might see herself' laughed Marianna.

'Yes she'll like that' Steve chuckled. 'But let's go inside.'

They entered the porch, which was like a small stone room with a sloping roof of limestone slates. It was cold and dark, serving as protection for the large wooden front door and as a connecting link between the secular and spiritual worlds.

Steve pushed the heavy door open and motioned to Marianna to go ahead. They were immediately assailed by a gloomy darkness. The artificial lights were wholly inadequate and the struggling natural light could only peep opaquely from the high clerestory windows. At the far end of the nave the light which entered through the chancel's stained glass had a delicate beauty, but it was hopelessly inadequate in soothing the general semblance of dismal melancholy. Marianna shivered.

'In front of us, here at the west end, is a Norman font which has some amazing carving' said Steve. 'It survived over the centuries because the carvings look like a farm scene, and therefore couldn't offend anyone during the destruction of the Reformation. But scholars have since identified it as a twelfth century image of hell, and you can see the plaited and interlaced patterns around the images which were used in most Norman sculpture.

'Now, look at the fan-vaulted roof. It's spectacular in such a small church and shows that this area was really important in medieval times.'

They walked slowly down the nave until they came to the mural of sinners being cast into hell. Steve stood back, waiting for Marianna's reaction. She stopped, speechless. The colours alone invoked suffering and torment, and the pictures of naked sinners being cast down the ladder from heaven where they were met by monsters and then cast cruelly into the flames of hell for perpetual torment were themselves a fearful vision, a dire warning of punishment.

'You see in the middle near the top we have Christ making the Last Judgement as he reads the book of life' Steve resumed. 'He is arranging the ascension of the saved and the fall of the damned. You can see the burial places opening with bodies forcing their way out. Some skeletons are complete, while others have had all their flesh removed. Some are still in their burial shrouds and those near the top are already in flight up to heaven. But get closer, see the faces of the damned. They are being dragged down into an endless night of fires, eternal punishment and torture from unimaginable monsters.'

Marianna turned to look at him. There was an expression of fascination on his face; relish, almost.

'You can see their fear' Steve continued. 'The sins of the world, greed, pride, envy and so on, are all clear. This would have been a terrifying picture for the uneducated peasants of medieval times. In those days reading was very rare, so the church communicated by pictures.'

Marianna shivered again. In the half-light she had noticed a row of corbels in the shapes of animal faces from Celtic antiquity looking down upon the scene. They too bore witness to the agony of hell and gave an energy and a power to the horror. Marianna moved closer. 'These pictures are like the works of Hieronymus Bosch' she said. 'But they are more fearful because of their setting.'

'But one of the most amazing things about this church is

the sheer scale of pagan symbols' interjected Steve. 'Look at the ends of the benches. Do you recognise this one?'

'Oh yes I do, it's like the pub sign.'

'Exactly, the Green Man. The plants and foliage growing out of his mouth are a fertility symbol dedicated to the harvest, a pagan prayer for good crops. Nobody knows what his origins were, but he's believed to go back to the Iron Age, around 400 BC. And if you look at other benches you'll see all sorts of animals and birds. Look at this one. It's a pelican – the pelican symbolises the resurrection. It's a mystery how the carvers knew what a pelican looked like in those days.'

'Maybe the climate was a lot hotter then. I can see what look like vines everywhere.'

'Yes that could be right. There are even some parrots.'

They moved further down the nave, dazzled by the sheer scale and number of the panels. They were on the walls, the floor, the pew ends, the pulpit and the rood screen, the seats for the choir, even behind the pillars. Most of them were harrowing, a warning to avoid sin. All had been designed to create fear in the unquestioning, unworldly medieval mind.

'They still work, don't they?' observed Steve quietly, looking at Marianna, whose colour had drained.

'Above the pulpit, that arch and its carvings. What are they?'

'OK, at the top is a knight on a horse slaying a dragon, so we know this church was dedicated to St George. The dragon is a representation of the devil. Below that we have seven little carved scenes. The numbers are mystical, but let's look at the pictures first. They are all carvings telling the story of Jesus' childhood. In the first we see the Annunciation, where the Angel Gabriel tells Mary that she is to be the mother of God. Then in the next one we see the Nativity, the birth of Jesus. We then see the shepherds being told of the birth, and that's followed by the adoration of the Three Wise Men, although I believe, strangely enough, that the bible doesn't say there were three. Then as a young man Jesus is presented to the Temple, where Simeon recognises him as the Messiah. We then see two final panels about the baptism.

'But the way this is structured is really important too. We have seven panels, God created the world in seven days and the repetition of seven-day weeks is like a constant run of musical notes in a scale. This was further proof in the medieval mind of divine geometry, which was supposed to be a godly master plan where everything was perfect, until the fall when Adam and Eve introduced evil. Are you bored yet?'

'No no, just cold, but this is fascinating. But again there's no proof of all this.'

'It's called faith' Steve laughed. He pulled her closer to share his warmth. She moved in to him cautiously, tucking her shoulder under his arm.

'And the numbers go on. Seven can be divided into four and three - four gospels and the three of the Holy Trinity. in fact many religious works and even carved faces have three sides. And there are seven virtues, which we see in many religious works. The three theological virtues of hope, faith and charity we read about in the bible in St Paul's letters. The remaining four are the cardinal virtues of temperance, prudence, fortitude and justice. Even prudence often has three faces - the past, present and future. It was Plato who said that the perfect person should possess the four cardinal virtues. And of course don't forget the seven deadly sins.

'You mentioned Hieronymus Bosch. Well he did a wonderful picture of these which is hanging in the Prado, in Madrid. And there were seven core subjects which the educated medieval mind would have studied - grammar, rhetoric and logic and the sciences of arithmetic, geometry, music and astronomy. And there are seven vices, opposite to the virtues. The list is endless, but you can go further. Four multiplied by three equals twelve. There are twelve months in the year, there were twelve tribes of Israel, there were twelve apostles... But let's move on and look at some more carvings.'

'There is just too much to understand. Suddenly I am seeing things which I have never noticed before.'

'Yes, you are looking at so much history, so much symbolism. Do you see those little stone corbels? They have a Celtic history. Remember, religion, or magic were all about nature before the Romans arrived. Here we have dogs, rabbits, a raven, cattle. They were missed by the reformers when they did so much damage. Sheer vandalism. You can see where the faces of the saints have been chipped off the body of the pulpit - they weren't acceptable either, and they were too obvious to be missed. All idolatrous images had to be destroyed. But let's move down towards the altar and the stained glass window.'

'It's so dark in here. Why didn't they make bigger windows?'

113

'The walls had to be very strong to support the roof, and they couldn't be weakened by too many windows. This is why they are small and high. And glass was very expensive. But there is also a dark logic in having a House of God which is sombre and fearful, because it keeps a sense of awe, especially in the medieval mind.'

A frisson crept down Marianna's spine; she felt that the fear was still very much alive. She was discovering that timeless connection to the past which is available only to those who can span the void of history. She was starting to sense that many speak the words, but few understand the language.

'So here we have the pulpit, which has many religious carvings. We can see Adam and Eve leaving Paradise, and there are the usual stories about the birth of Christ. Just opposite is the lectern where readings from the bible take place, you can see it's built on an eagle, which is the symbol of St John, who was a preacher. And all over the walls are memorial plaques. They help us to remember the dead, but they also warn us that we too will die and face judgement with an eternity in heaven or hell, a real inspiration to lead a godly life.'

'There's just too much to take in.'

'And I'm only pointing out the obvious things. As you get used to the church you'll notice all sorts of strange symbolism. For instance hidden on the wall behind the lectern is a quatrefoil design which goes back to the days of alchemy. It possibly represents the four phases of the moon, or it might represent the four elements, air, earth, fire and water. And this is where it gets interesting, because these should have been destroyed in the reformation. These four elements have spirits which live in them and go back to ancient pagan beliefs. Some believe that the spirits are the remains of evil people who can't move on, while others believe they represent a lower order of human. Others split them into angels, higher spirits, and devils, lower spirits. The nature and personalities of these spirits were first described in antiquity, so it's really amazing to see something like this surviving. It smells of witchcraft and the occult.

'It certainly does' murmured Marianna.

'And now as we move closer to the altar we also get closer to God. Many churches didn't allow ordinary people into the chancel. It represents heaven, so it was only open to the priests. But we can go in.' He motioned to her to ascend the steps into the chancel. 'Just look at this beautiful rood screen with all the carvings. This screen represents the division of the earth, which is the nave where we are now, and heaven, where the altar is. You see we have to walk up three steps to get to the chancel? This tells us that the chancel has higher status. The church is full of symbolism like this. And when we go to the crypt we will go downstairs, because it has lower status. You can see the altar is a relatively simple affair. It represents the table from the last supper. The only carvings it has are the ten commandments on the surface facing the body of the church.'

'But some churches have circular altars in the middle, so they are closer to the worshippers?'

'Yes, but not here. This altar was placed under the stained glass window to draw people's attention to the story of Jesus. This was to educate the largely illiterate population. They couldn't read, but they could certainly understand a picture. It caused quite a stir at the time, because the bible states that images of God should not be allowed, but education was deemed to be more important than a strict biblical interpretation. Although the iconoclasm of the reformation did try to return to the original purity.

'Now, in this window we see the central theme of the Crucifixion, with the Virgin and St John looking up at the Cross. This in itself is a remarkable image which would never have been allowed in the other two monotheistic religions, Judaism and Islam. And then in all these other panels we see the seven days of the creation leading up to the Fall from Eden, with the expulsion of Adam and Eve. You can see how compelling this would have been to the illiterate peasants of medieval times.'

Marianna stood back and looked up in awe. The light gently diffusing through the images not only gave a glorious backdrop to the colour but sent shafts of light dancing into the body of the chancel. The figures and the illuminated story seemed to glow softly, a gentle lantern of knowledge and devotion. They brought a tranquillity which contrasted sharply with her earlier feelings of fear and disquiet.

'Now, behind the altar there is a door which drops down to a spiral staircase to the catacombs. It's not quite so much fun down there.'

CHAPTER ELEVEN

Marianna gritted her teeth. She knew the pleasant part of the tour was over.

CHAPTER TWELVE

As Steve pulled a big old-fashioned key from his coat pocket and moved towards the heavy wooden door behind the altar, Marianna stood frozen to the spot. It seemed to her for a moment that she could see a grey shape standing sentinel around the door, as if it were shrouded in a blanket or a cloak. It gave off a semblance of menace. Even as she looked, it faded – her over-stimulated imagination, clearly. But when she looked to the side, she could see it again, out of the corner of her eye. She shuddered.

'Everything all right?' Clearly Steve had seen nothing.

'Hey, come and help, this key won't turn' he went on. 'The lock must be rusted from lack of use. Nobody goes down here very often.'

'It's dicky, like locks at the Manor. Jiggle it up and down a bit' she offered.

'I beg your pardon?' Steve laughed, giving her a cheeky grin. She turned away in embarrassment. What on earth had she said that for?

As she moved towards the door the greyness seemed to

dissolve and disappear, as if it had been sucked into the fabric of the church. Gently she grasped the key and eased it in. It turned effortlessly. It was as if she alone were being invited in.

'It is welcoming you' said Steve, with a grin. She shuddered.

The door swung inwards, hinges creaking in protest, sending their message of alarm echoing down the stairwell into the subterranean gloom where only silence and darkness lived in comfortable union with the spirits of the dead. The stone steps wound down before them and the light of Steve's torch flickered and reflected off the damp surfaces of the walls. The surface of each step had a curved fatigue where countless boots had worn away the surface over the centuries.

Steve led the way, his torch driving a path through the darkness and creating fantastical shapes on the walls around them, shapes which Marianna chose not to examine too closely. The shaft of light from the torch conjured up a fearful shifting picture of shapes and shadows. She saw beasts from hell; faces of terror against the wall which instantly disappeared, to be replaced by contorted animals with heads of deadly teeth and evil searching eyes. Their claws flexed in anticipation of pain and destruction, their tails thrashed in anger and aggression. In her mind, flames of banishment and retribution were fed by a cascade of naked bodies in a Satanic fuel of sin. The very soundlessness of it all increased the terror.

Her feet brought her to an abrupt halt; they had reached the bottom. She found herself standing on a flat stone floor with a dark passage stretching away into the gloom. It was a seemingly endless tunnel into darkness, with jagged flint walls supporting curved arches built from broken red brick. Shadows recoiled from the intrusion and then leapt back as they passed. The whole structure groaned with damp and mould, looking as if at any moment it would give up the struggle to hold back the tons of sodden earth above and collapse upon them, burying them and the tunnel's secrets for ever. The smell of decay and undisturbed age hinted at an enclosed world of isolation.

Marianna gasped and jumped back in fright. A tiny scuttling sound amplified by the walls disturbed the silence as a rat, looking monstrous in the torchlight, scurried past; it was heading not away from them but towards them, as if some terror far greater than that of mortal humans was propelling it. Only a sweep of Steve's boot diverted it back into the shadows.

'Are you all right?' asked Steve. 'Come along the passage a little way. Look here now.' He moved a few feet ahead and directed the torch to one side. 'These are the rooms where the bones of the dead were stacked and stored. When the church was built they disturbed the pagan remains, but they have all been saved and stored.'

Marianna was weak with fear, but she was determined not to show it. 'Yes, I'm OK' she said faintly. She stepped closer to Steve and gripped his arm. She wasn't sure she trusted him, but at least he was living flesh and blood.

'In this first room you can see the stone sarcophagi' he said, shining the torch to show her. 'They were used for hundreds of years to hold the bodies of some of our local leaders. This is the only room where the walls were decorated, though many of the early Christian images have perished over the years. But there are also many pagan signs.' He flashed the torch to show her some vague shapes on the walls. 'Their meanings are unclear, but we think they were put in as an apology, almost an insurance for disturbing the ancient relics.'

She peered warily into the room, wishing she had brought her own torch. The chamber was stacked with dozens of stone coffins three high, many with ornate carvings, apparently referring to Old Testament stories. She turned back to follow Steve down the tunnel. It appeared to be getting very slightly narrower and lower as they moved along it, and it seemed to Marianna that the walls were starting to close in and the ceiling was descending as if to crush the interlopers. As she thought this there sounded a gentle whisper around her head: voices, yet not quite voices; human, yet less than human. They seemed to be issuing a soft invitation to stay, to merge, to be a part of a great mystery which could promise so much.

She shook herself, trying to banish the feelings. As she did so the voices seem to be silenced, only to crowd in on her again within moments.

She followed Steve along the passage, wishing that he would not insist on continuing. Yet his appetite for this world of death seemed to know no bounds.

'Look at this one' he said, grinning. She peered along the torch beam to see that this room contained – horror of horrors

– human skulls. Hundreds of skulls. They were neatly stacked, their empty eyes staring back at the interlopers, their ghastly teeth grinning a welcome. Those at the top seemed clean and fresh, as if their owners had died only yesterday, while those at the bottom were yellowed and grimy with age. One of them seemed to have a string of flesh extending out of an eye socket, but then, as Marianna watched, she saw it twitch. It was the tail of a rat. She gasped in fear.

'We should not be here' she said. 'We are not wanted here. We should go back now.'

'Oh no, this is far too interesting' said Steve. 'Can't let a few rats stop us.'

In the next chamber a pile of bones had been stacked.

'Human femurs' said Steve. Marianna wondered how he knew so much about it.

'Skulls, leg bones what did they do with the rest? she asked.

By way of response Steve pointed the torch into the next room. This one contained piles of breastbones, fibulas, tibias, humerus bones, arm and hand bones, all seeming to be waiting for reunion with one another. Who had butchered the owners of these poor relics? Had it been done after death – or before? Marianna tried to throw off this gruesome thought. Everywhere was an atmosphere of cold, damp and despair.

In one room, Steve pointed up towards the ceiling.

'Do you see that plaque, covered in dust and grime? If you look very carefully you will see EZ37 written on it. Nobody knew what this was until some scholar came down here about fifty years ago. He suggested that it refers to chapter 37 of the

Old Testament book of Ezekiel. This seemed to solve the mystery, because that passage quotes God himself in the field of bones: '*I will cause breath to enter you, and you shall live. I will lay sinews on you, and will cause flesh to come upon you, and cover you with skin, and put breath in you and you shall live.*' So what you see is a very real presumption of the Resurrection.'

Marianna was speechless. There was more to this than she had ever contemplated.

They moved on, looking into one storage vault after another. All the time Steve kept up his eager commentary. It was as if he relished the fear and felt his talking would show defiance to the shadows and the ethereal illusions which threatened to engulf them. He seemed remarkably at home down here, Marianna thought.

But then her concentration wavered; she had started to feel a gradual warmth around her, one of sensuality and security. It was as if a bubble of protection was being created, with her at the centre. Her body began to relax. She felt the onset of a gentle glow, a tingling sincerity and compassion which she had never known before. And the whispering voices of welcome had returned; a gentle seductive breath; an intimate suggestion which sighed itself into the most receptive parts of her brain.

'I wonder who this chap was' said Steve. He was looking at another skull; a large, well-preserved one, placed at eye level upon a stand in an alcove. Marianna looked at it and almost, it seemed to her, it stared back. Was it her imagination, or had it turned very slightly to face her?

And while she stared at the skull, wisps and tendrils of

contact started. She felt fingertip touches of gentleness all over her body. There was a soft but firm stroking around her head and neck; gentle fingers moved through her hair, and ran down her shoulders and back. And they were massaging her legs too; moving up past her thighs and buttocks to her stomach and breasts. The touches were remorseless and compelling. She stood there in compliance while the whisper-voices breathed submission. And the stroking produced a rapport where her body took over and a yielding to the instinct seemed right. Now somehow the fingers were inside her clothes with their gossamer tips covering her entire body; constantly caressing and sweeping her skin. And the sensitivity started to go deeper into her flesh as her breasts began to stir with their nipples testing the tightness of their captivity. And she felt her breathing slowly getting deeper, but faster as her heartbeat began to race; and all the while the insistent intensity of those silky fingers continued their exploration. They were everywhere, until finally she moved her weight slightly onto her left leg while her right leg slid away to open. And those relentless fingers were following so gently; they seemed to know. And other fingers were bringing pressure on the front of her soft panties in a pull and relax motion which gave a gentle friction to that most sensitive part of her body, a movement which was constantly repeated while other fingers and what felt like moist tongues were separating and penetrating. Then suddenly she stiffened as her whole body tensed and her muscles contracted again and again while she fell into the abyss. And the whispering kept commanding her mind; but then softly faded away.

'Hey, are you listening to me?' Steve interrupted. She stared at him, speechless, lips glistening, eyes shining. Steve stared at her. He looked at the skull. Then he took a step closer to her.

'He has yet the power' he muttered in a low undertone. He lifted her chin and covered her mouth with his. She stiffened and tried to move back, to push him away as this was different. He did not understand - this was not what she wanted, not at all. This harshness, the lack of sensitivity and finesse was a bewildering contrast to what had just happened.

She felt numb in horror.

'*Now I have my proof*' she thought.

'It's OK Steve' she said in a quiet reflection. 'I am fine, just feel a little strange. So much death! Take me back, please.'

He stared at her for a moment, then led her back towards the spiral stairway. There was no more running commentary.

CHAPTER THIRTEEN

'Come on Ben! If you want to come, hurry up' shouted Alison. 'Marianna has already left for the church and Trixie and Vadoma are leaving now.'

'OK!' Ben tore down the stairs in a melée of dogs, all shouting and barking, and piled into the car in a confusion of legs and bodies. It was just a short drive to the blacksmith's, via the Co-op to help get the shopping, and Ben disembarked almost before the car had stopped and raced through the gate, past the half-doors and into the furnace-hell of the smithy.

'Whoa, slow down!' Mr Bevin was fashioning some iron gates, with firework explosions of sparks which completely stopped Ben in his tracks, his eyes speechless from surprise. 'Keep away! These'll hurt if they hit you' warned the smith. 'We'll go to see Mr Chilcott later, so he can make you a real leather apron like mine. And we have Farmer Salter coming soon with two horses needing shoes. So there's lots to do today.'

As they were talking, the Salter horsebox drove up and parked opposite the front gate. 'Go and help unload, and take them to the yard at the back' instructed Mr Bevin. Ben needed no more instructions, and dashed across the road.

'Good morning Mr Salter.'

'Mornin' young Ben.' The ramp of the truck was quickly let down and the two horses ambled out with country *sangfroid*. 'We've been here before' they seemed to say to each other as they strolled down on to the road. They obviously knew where to go, so Ben walked with them to the yard, tucked behind the smithy.

'Tie 'em to the rails and close the gate' said Mr Salter as he drove off.

'We won't see him for a while, Green Man mos' likely' laughed Mr Bevin.

Back in the Smithy, Mr Bevin started to explain some of the arts of the smith to his young visitor. 'You see those horseshoes? They started out as flat bars of iron which have been curved to fit the hoof. Then holes are put in for the nails. We heat them up and press them on to the foot, then nail them on when we see they fit. It doesn't hurt the horse. Stand back and watch. You see how I run my hand down the horse's leg? that tells him to raise his leg so I can get to the foot. These horses are well trained, they stand still so they're easy to shoe. You hold the nails and hand them to me when I ask for them.'

'Can I try?'

'Not yet' laughed Mr Bevin. 'It takes years to learn. If you get it wrong you damage the horse. But watch carefully. First I take off the old shoe. See how worn down it is? Then I get my knife and cut away any uneven growth. Has to be good and sharp. Then I smooth the hoof with the rasp.' But when he looked around, Mr Bevin found that neither the knife nor the rasp were where they should have been.

'Strange things bin happening lately. Things being moved around. Must be they damn poltergeists.' He laughed. 'Leave the horses here, we'll go inside and get what we need.'

As man and boy walked through the back door, there came a new urgency. There was a sudden feeling of pent-up energy, although nothing had obviously changed from earlier; a semblance of brooding upheaval. It was as if a child being present had vitalised some dormant force which like an invisible cloud was awakening...

And then it started.

On the darkly-stained heavy oak table by the furnace, a hammer began to rattle and dance on the surface. The hammer lifted up, brushing aside pieces of scrap iron and moving towards the edge of the table. It fell to the floor with a clang.

'Will you look at that!' breathed Mr Bevin.

But that was just the beginning. Now other tools started to oscillate and the unfinished gate itself began to vibrate. In the far corner, a glass-fronted cupboard suddenly exploded with a force which projected glass shards all over the room. The nails which were carefully boxed inside it shot across the room like a salvo of arrows, somehow all flying point first.

Ben froze. The farrier, who was leading, collapsed with a groan of shock and pain. He lay moaning on the floor, his arms and face a pincushion of glass and nails. His leather apron had saved the rest of his body.

'Get help, boy!' he groaned. Ben fled upstairs to the smith's flat. There was equal chaos there too. Furniture had been turned over and china and ornaments had been swept off the mantelpiece in an orgy of destruction. The carpet seemed to be undulating, sending small objects flying towards the windows. Ben found the telephone and picked it up, but there was no dialling tone. The lights surged on and off with no response to the switches.

Then a huge crash came from the yard. Ben ran down to see the farrier struggling out of the back door, wiping blood from his face and eyes. The chimney stack had collapsed into the yard, covering it with rubble and blocking his path to the horses, which were pushing hard at the gate to escape, their tranquil routine now a tempest of agitation driven by those ethereal forces which only animals are aware of. Their ears were flat and their eyes were white and rolling in terror. Then the gate opened, seemingly of its own accord - and they were gone.

Inside the chaos was increasing. All the doors and windows were now flying open against the walls and then slamming repeatedly shut. From upstairs a further crashing could be heard, of pictures falling off walls, doors and windows smashing open and shut, furniture sliding about.

Now the furnace joined in, blazing suddenly to white heat. Hot coals exploded in a deadly volley across the room, turning it into an inferno of heat, quickly setting fire to the wooden slats by the windows and then to the beams and work tables. Within seconds, fires were raging both upstairs and down. It was like a medieval scene where the flaming coals were a precursor to torturing the damned.

And with the sound of the fire gripping and grasping came a muffled sound; the sound of infernal laughter....or perhaps it was the rushing of wind being stoked by the turmoil.

'Ben, get out!' yelled Mr Bevin as he fought his way through the smoke, the fumes and the blood now pumping from his wounds. They struggled through the back door to look back and see the fires of hell itself. Flames were bullying and destroying the roof and the structure of the building; crimson and yellow hands beckoned through the windows with teasing fingers which emerged from the smoky cover urging them to come back; to come closer and be absorbed. It seemed to Ben that the fire was talking to him, a gentle whisper of gratitude behind the manic chuckling, thanking him for his energy, the energy which had released the playful spirit of destruction.

* * * * * *

At the Green Man four old gaffers were sitting in the sun getting better acquainted with several pints of scrumpy.

'Lor a'mighty, there be my 'orses' said Farmer Salter in a shocked voice as his beloved animals cantered on to the village green. 'Better catch 'em.'

They sprang to their feet and hobbled out on to the green as best they could, given the effects of age and the scrumpy. Looking over the roof of the pub they saw a tall column of black smoke in the general direction of the smithy. Without a word, they broke into a run. They arrived outside the smithy in company with the rest of the village, who were standing shocked at the sight of the building being voraciously consumed by a spitting and crackling inferno. There was no sign of Mr Bevin or Ben.

'Ben!' shouted Alison. Heedless of the flames, she charged in through the front door. She could see no one in the forge, so she rushed towards the stairs. As she got closer the acrid smoke began to make breathing more difficult and the heat seemed to be burning the inside of her lungs. The paint on the walls was getting discoloured and was starting to blister, and sharp talons of flame reached towards her from unseen holes grasping to capture and kill. It was as if a mind was controlling their aggression. And they kept poking up through the gaps in the floorboards; shimmering hands with elongated fingers, ready to seize greedily; to kiss and withdraw. Ready to play again.

At the top of the stairs she was met by a wall of flame and heat advancing from the back end of the landing. She pushed on into the front room, sobbing with fear for her son.

All the time the smoke was getting thicker, while the sharp crackling of the flames seemed to be amplified, mingling in her mind with a ghoulish laughter at her streaming tears, at her smoke and soot covered body. The flames had now advanced further, and had such a firm grip that the snapping and popping of tinder-dry wood gave, in her confused and oxygen-starved body, an orchestral harmony to the terror which was almost soothing in its finality. She could hear the explosions and cannons of an approaching army, like a Tchaikovskyesque salute to the final moments. But still she struggled against her fate.

'Think girl, think!' she whispered; and then, in a far corner, she saw a linen cupboard. Inside would be sheets and blankets which could be made into a rope – but there was no time. The door to the landing was in flames and she felt her strength leaving her. All her reserves had been used up with the constant coughing; the crying of smoke-punished tears made her eyes sting and unable to see clearly. Her senses were lurching from reality to visions of Ben, and she found herself imagining a horrific picture of a blackened mass of burnt flesh without identity, which she was unable to rescue. Through all this it seemed that the flames had become human. She saw a pair of evil, malicious eyes and heard scorning laughter, mocking her efforts. But it had to be the crackling of the timber and the shimmering lights from the flames playing with her tortured mind.

Then she heard the shout. 'They're at the back! get out QUICKLY!' She turned to run, but the flames had advanced too far. Below she heard the siren of a fire engine.

It was too late. It was time to embrace death, embrace her dead son in another place. She sank slowly to the floor, as if embracing her fate. Oblivion would be a welcome release from this hell of smoke and heat. She was only very dimly aware of voices, of shapes coming through the windows, of being seized in strong arms and bundled up to be carried to safety. Now Ben was hugging her and crying and telling her... she knew not what. She passed out.

CHAPTER FOURTEEN

It was a wonderful morning to walk to the gypsy site. A gentle breeze was whispering over the meadows and the morning sun was caressing life back from winter hibernation. As Vadoma and Trixie left the house they headed towards the potholed path behind the church, which led softly down through an old oak wood. These ancient giants backed on to the graveyard and led down to the stream which fed into the estuary. The pair quickly entered a hushed world of twilight, where the tangle of branches embraced above their heads to produce a shaded, cool umbrella under which the path rambled in an apparently aimless zigzag down the gradual slope.

Shafts of sunlight were smiling through the canopy which produced an entrancing variegated avenue stretching ahead which illuminated on the woodland floor the russet browns of last year's leaves, whose dry brittleness was slowly mulching down in an unselfish offering to the rest of nature. There were the sharp greens of huge colonies of moss on the embankments which supported a confusion of young trees and shrubs; and shade-loving plants were cautiously emerging from their winter sleep while bright flashes of yellow daffodils celebrated their escape from suburbia.

The silence was broken, if you stopped and listened carefully, by the rustlings of small animals, the harsh cries of cock pheasants and the hypnotic melody of courting woodpigeons. Hidden deeper in the woods were the small birds which moved from branch to branch in the timeless hunt for insects, and in the distance echoed the occasional rat-a-tat of the woodpecker, always keeping tantalisingly out of sight. Among the larger trees were mixed brambles, hawthorn, beech and holly, all combining to provide shelter and protection to the forest dwellers. But it was the oaks, the kings of the forest, with the age and grandeur in their twisted trunks and branches which inspired stories of a different, generally unseen, human dimension.

'Is this where the fairies and forest people live?' asked Trixie. 'Florika says that we can go and look for them.'

'Oh yes' enthused Vadoma. 'Did she tell you all about the different types? There are good and bad ones.'

The conversation batted back and forth until suddenly they had left the trees behind and a vast landscape of open moorland, swamp and wetlands stretched before them. They stood on a small and crumbling ancient hump-backed bridge which crossed the main river. It was the perfect spot from which to admire the view - even that extra few feet of height gave distance to the panorama.

They saw a magical misty landscape where the veil of the early-morning haze was starting to dissipate to reveal an estuary pulsing with life. While some creatures were returning to their homes and burrows exhausted from the nightly conflict with death, others were starting out to feed, noses and whiskers twitching, tiny eyes and fragile hands darting here and there, not only watching for danger but searching for signs of prey.

'Look how the trees and shrubs seem to be floating on the water' said Vadoma. The mist gently resting on the surface gave an opaque cloak to the roots and trunks which remained hidden in the swirling greyness. Only the tops poked out, like an ethereal jungle waving in the soft breeze.

'I can imagine the fairies would like to live here' said Trixie in a serious tone of voice which brought a smile to Vadoma's eyes. 'Come on, hurry up. Let's find Florika.' She pointed to the animal trail which skirted the estuary and led to the gypsy site a few hundred yards away. There was the shallow water's edge on the one side with a jumble of willows fighting for room with ash, alder and hawthorn bushes on the other. The water was home to a vast area of reed beds and sedges which provided a safe haven for countless birds and small animals, while further out the streams all merged into a constantly changing pattern of sand bars and mud flats. But Trixie only had eyes for her friend, who was waiting by the gate which kept the animals within the confines of the site.

'Hi Trixie, hi Vad!' 'Hi Flo!' Greetings all round. 'We need to go to see your family. There have been some odd things happening lately.' Dodging the piled up-pallets and a variety of discarded rubbish, they found their way to Esmeralda's caravan. She needed to warn Vadoma about where not to go, as there were several large pools and tidal flats which were dangerous.

'Just keep to the shore and in the woods and you'll be OK, but don't go too far' said Esmeralda, echoing the ill-appreciated instructions of parents everywhere. Having offered tea and biscuits to anybody who showed, they soon attracted a friendly crowd of about fifteen people, all talking together and giving advice about where to go to see the fairies. 'But you must be quiet… they are easily frightened.' Trixie's eyes were wide with anticipation as they set off, Vadoma ambling along too, though she was on a separate mission - to note any rare plants for Granny, especially an accessible source of mistletoe, that most sacred of protectors.

'Flo, if you see any magic plants like angelica, ash or rowan let me know.'

'Oh yes… we'll miss the angelica as that grows by the water and we are going into the woods, but there are lots of rowan trees in the glade where we're heading. We collect it and put it outside our homes to keep the witches away, they hate the red berries!' She laughed.

'That's fantastic.' Trixie's mind was already expanding into the impossible.

'We need to go deep into the wildwoods where the evergreens grow. They give protection to the fairies over the winter, so they make their homes there.'

'How many have you seen? Are they all the same?' enthused Trixie, eyes wide, desperately trying to believe.

'Well, I haven't seen very many' Florika said, almost truthfully. 'But they are definitely there, and there are many different types. If we see any tall ragwort plants, sometimes they have treasure buried underneath the roots and the fairies fly on the stalks to get around. And we have some hobgoblins to help around the house and look after the village, but they are so ugly that they hide, so people can't see them. If you give them clothes then they will leave, so they are always naked as well'.

'Yuk' from Trixie.

'But there are nasty ones too. Goblins are always picking fights and they can change shape to hurt people. We had one in the village who was very beautiful but really she was a vampire. She got chased out after she was seen sucking a man dry of blood after she had killed him.'

Trixie stopped in horror. 'We won't see any of those, will we?' she asked in trepidation. Yet in the back of her mind was a curiosity, a trembling sense of anticipation and hope, as if she wished to court danger and explore the unknown. Which was fine, as long as she wasn't alone.

'We might do' said Florika with a wicked grin. 'But the ones we are looking for today are the spirits of streams, lakes and woods. They were living before the church and the village were here.'

'That's right' added Vadoma. 'Steve from the pub said that they had descended from the pagan gods. But he thinks that they were very upset when the church got built because they had their own religious site there. So we have to be careful.'

'That must be why water spirits sometimes try to drown humans. But the ones we want to look out for are the tree spirits who live among the oak trees. They are very friendly, unless their trees are cut down. We had a man who cut down some trees for winter firewood but he died soon after when his house burnt down. His three small children disappeared and we think the tree spirits took them to look after them. So they are very kind really. We will see the biggest and oldest oak tree in the forest – it's in the clearing.'

And so, with their backs to the estuary, they started trekking through the Wildwoods. There was a criss-cross pattern of seemingly random paths used by hidden and secretive animals, and, as they got deeper into the gloom the trees became bigger and darker. There were oaks, sycamores, beech, alder, all scrambling to the sky and the light, which produced an aerial energy-grasping carpet. There was an understorey of bushes and shrubs such as hazel and holly which provided food and shelter for the smaller birds and animals. This was the strange harmony within the violence of nature, where sanctuary and nutrition were provided from the forest floor, up through the smaller shrubs to the canopy itself.

'Keep your eyes open for the small people' whispered Vadoma. 'They live in the undergrowth, under mushrooms and toadstools and in the hollows of old trees. There are elves, gnomes, tree spirits and spirits of the dead who have chosen to come back. And there are spirits of earth, sea, sky and fire. Some are very mischievous and others work sinister magic. They live in nature itself, but not many humans can see them.' Florika nodded in agreement; she had been raised with the same gypsy lore. Trixie's eyes were wide in anticipation, and a little fear. Nothing in her background had prepared her for this.

The trees now had a more sinister air. There was a slightly threatening feeling, as if the wood was watching them; a sense of quiet expectation. When a roe deer suddenly broke cover and went crashing off through the undergrowth, they all jumped in shock.

'Are you sure you know where we are, Florika?' asked Vadoma.

'Yes, we'll be in the glade soon where the Great Oak is' she replied.

They thrust their way on through the green gloom. As they walked the shrubs seemed to part to allow their passage and then to close firmly again behind them, so when they looked back they could see no path, no way back.

At last they came to the glade. It was a small grassy dell guarded by a ring of tall trees all around it. In the centre was an enormous oak. No longer graceful, its massive bole was the size of a house. The girls knew that here at least they were safe. The great tree gave out a feeling of strength, solidarity and goodness. All their recent misgivings were banished.

This ancient tree had long been father to the forest, a home and provider to all manner of small animals and birds, beetles, wasps and flies, butterflies and moths, lichens, fungi and ivy. Beneath the outer fringes was a mass of colour from bluebells, wood anemones, primroses and sorrel, plants which depended on the circle of light around the great tree for their survival.

'We must be very quiet now. We sit under the tree and wait. Take some of this' said Vadoma as she passed around a flask. 'It is some of Esmeralda's special pick-me-up potion which she gave me before we left.'

They took it in turns to drink from the flask. The liquid was a thick concoction of honey, mead and other strange-smelling substances which produced an instant physical lethargy but released the mind into a heightened awareness. Suddenly, with a great sense of happiness and relief, they saw activity which hitherto had been hidden. The old oak tree was suddenly alive with miniature figures, and they saw its many cracks and holes, now clearly the homes of the tiny tree spirits. There were winged fairies who ducked and dived around the heads of larger pixies and imps, which were tall, thin and angular with pointed noses and ears. They were too slow-moving to bat away their tormentors, who were, after all, just having fun. There was activity everywhere and movement around the flowers and toadstools as hordes of multi-coloured fairies played in the sunlight.

The three humans were mesmerised. For what felt like hours they were unable to move, thanks to Esmeralda's potion.

But it couldn't last.

Without warning the sun disappeared and a dark shadow filled the gap in the trees. Suddenly the glade was a cold and hostile place. All the fairy activity ceased as if a switch had been thrown. They felt the great oak tree sigh; once again its strength was to be tested.

'Come on, we must get back, it looks like rain' said Vadoma. She got up and started to lead the way back down the path they had come from.

'That's not the way' said Florika. 'It's over there.' She pointed at the darkest and densest part of the surrounding woodland; the beginning of a very rough path could be seen.

'Are you sure? OK, you'd better lead, you know these woods.' But they seemed to be going in the wrong direction.

As they dived into the bushes, some strange intuition prodded Vadoma to glance up, yet again, at the sky. Above the canopy hung a strange black cloud. And it seemed to be approaching them. Soon it completely filled the heavens, churning and rolling with strange shapes. She saw faces, gargoyle faces…

And then came the lightning. Brilliant, deadly eyes of fire seemed to flash from the churning cloud. Raging faces spat vitriol towards earth. Thunder crashing directly above them, they fled deeper into the safety of the trees as fast as they could.

Vadoma knew they had been discovered by forces too powerful to take on, forces with which modern man had lost all connection. It seemed that even the woods had turned cruel and hostile. The path kept fading out and they had to push onwards through prickling bushes with pitiless thorns which extended their claws towards them to stab and tear. The branches seemed to lash out as the girls passed, like waiting feline predators. Trixie and Florika were soon in tears.

The trio were now soaked, for dense rain had begun to pour

through the branches, and blood was seeping everywhere from cuts and pricks. In their panic and fear they started running. Now darkness began to close in. The shadows were getting bolder and moving closer from the trees on both sides. The branches, twisted and warped with evil, seemed to be reaching down in a tangled net to snare and abduct, while overhead the remorseless Armageddon of thunder and the hell-light of the flashes from the malicious clouds filled them with numbing fear.

'Stop!' shouted Vadoma to the two girls. 'This no good! We are lost. We need to find shelter. Quickly – in here.' In front of them was a gigantic black jagged splinter of an ancient blasted oak, the stark and rotting corpse of a once majestic tree. Vadoma was pointing to a deep, dark hollow at its base.

And then a miracle. Lights – the lights of torches.

'They find us!' shouted Vadoma, barely audible above the wind and rain. They left the shelter and ran towards the lights, which seemed to be bobbing towards them. But as they got closer they realised that something was wrong; the lights seemed to be getting no nearer, and their shouts died on the wind, with no answering voices. If the lights were not the torches of a search party, what could they be?

They ran on, the lights ever seeming to recede before them, until suddenly, without warning, they felt an abrupt change in the ground underfoot. The hard woodland floor had given way to a wet, soft, slimy mud which threatened to suck their feet down and hold them fast. Florika knew they were in the swamp which surrounded the Dark Pool, where insidious tidal currents had caused the deaths of many local fishermen. It was an area treated with superstitious dread. And now they could smell the dank reek of rotting kelp; the sea.

Somehow they had moved in a circle. But now they had another problem to contend with; mist. It hung over the land in the gathering dark, masking god-knows-what further dangers which lay ahead. Far above them they heard the cries of gulls, exulting that three more travellers had come to perish in the Grey Swamp. It was a desolate cry, the last sound heard by generations of sailors lost at sea. An awful smell of decomposition washed around them as they pulled themselves out of the mud. But still the lights hung there, a little way ahead of them, a tantalising temptation to seek safety.

'Where are we? What are those lights?' sobbed Trixie through chattering teeth. She was now thoroughly frightened and shivering with cold.

Just then something touched her ankle; the tendril of some creeping, nameless swamp plant. It stretched before her feet like a snare waiting for the unwary. With a screech of shock, she lost her balance. As she fell towards the putrid swamp a ghastly face rose to meet her from the soggy depths. She landed beside that horror of bloated whiteness with the skull inches from her lips. The empty sockets were turned towards her, home to a fermenting mass of grubs which bubbled with fatness and greed. They writhed around the nostrils and pushed into the lipless mouth where the teeth were set in a permanent grin. The rest of the clothesless body was a mass of corruption with ribs partially covered in flesh which was being rendered from the bones in strips to be carried off by the swamp dwellers. The arms were tight to the body with hands like claws; fingers twisted and knotted as the flesh fell away. The abomination was surrounded by a squirming restlessness as the mud seethed with movement.

Trixie screamed again and again; the scream of the damned. She lay prostrate on the mud in terror, unable to take her eyes off the horror in front of her. Around her it seemed she could hear voices, calling her, taunting her, tempting her, terrifying her. Faint lights bobbed and glowed above the mud.

And now the dead, eyeless head moved. It arched its gap-toothed grin in a foul smile of blind, putrid death... and spoke in a deep, glutinous hiss.

'*Trixie...!*' it seemed to hiss... or it might have been the foul mud settling, the evil smelling gases easing their way to the surface in a whisper of escape.

She screamed again, and scrambled in desperation and terror to her feet.

Then at last they heard shouts – normal, human shouts. Now a barrage of voices sounded, calling their names. The seductive lights had disappeared, to be replaced by real ones, bobbing torchlights with the shapes of men behind them. A normal human face appeared in the mist, then another, and then Fonso and his men emerged from the gloom.

'Thank God we've found you. We saw the storm approaching. We've been searching for the last hour' said Fonso.

'We were following lights' said Vadoma. 'We think you come for us.'

Fonso had a look of extreme urgency. He scanned the swamp around them. 'What you saw were will o' the wisps, evil fairies' he said. 'They are dangerous spirits. They lead people into the swamps and then drown them as they get stuck. Who screamed?'

'Trixie found a body, that's why she scream.'

Trixie was standing, hugging herself, shivering and speechless with shock. One of the men picked her up to carry her back to safety.

Vadoma showed Fonso the spot where Trixie had fallen, but there was nothing to see. The mud was flat and featureless. There was no face, no trace of humanity or anything else. Only the putrid smell faintly lingered.

CHAPTER FIFTEEN

'It's amazing how quickly everyone has recovered' I observed to Alison some weeks later. The family was back to normal again. Granny was stumping crossly around the house waving her stick at any child who appeared to be making a noise. Alison's trauma was firmly behind her, no nonsense there.

'It's incredible how soon the past seems to be forgotten' I went on. 'Trixie and Ben have both left behind them what they saw. Children are so resilient.'

'Yes, but you know what always surprises me? Mum is up and about so quickly. The other day I heard her talking to Vadoma about the paranormal. She has so much knowledge. She was saying that spirits need lots of energy to be active. It's a bit like lizards and other cold-blooded animals that can't move very fast until they get warmth from the sun. Apparently solar storms make a big difference. She says solar flares bring an immense boost in energy and paranormals can use this. But I've no idea how it all works.'

'Apparently these storms do the same thing' I said. 'When Vad and Trixie were in the swamp, Vad said she could feel the earth rocking from the power of the noise and lightning. It took her back to her Romany childhood - they were never allowed to go out in such weather. Her family believed that the world was taken over by demons and ghosts at such times. This is why when you see a ghost you feel coldness. They suck all the heat and energy from the atmosphere to give them strength. Bit hard to swallow, though.'

'There was a full moon that night, as well' she went on. 'The vicar told me hospital admissions go up when there's a full moon, especially during cold weather.'

'Have you noticed that Marianna has been very quiet about these things lately?' I pointed out. 'I think Steve's been filling her mind with all sorts of stories. She seems to be hanging around with him a lot.'

'She's easily influenced, that girl. Maybe I should have a word with her, woman to woman.'

* * * * * *

Spring drifted quietly into summer, and for weeks the only strange sightings were those recorded by the less reliable clients of the Green Man on their unsteady progress home late at night.

Family life quickly returned to normal. As the summer term advanced the children became increasingly addicted to the internet. They had found a feverish anarchy of keyboards and subversion; a world where anyone over 16 had escaped from Jurassic Park. Trixie even rapturously lectured the Vicar on the merits of the Microchip Messiah with much pointing and clicking. He tried to explain that pointing was very rude, which was met with a stunned silence. He thought it was a silence of shame and was much relieved. As soon as they returned in the evenings they went on line, running rampant through an uncontrolled world and laughing at doomed adult ruses to protect them from the net's sordid recesses.

One day they found a story about a man who had 'had relations' with a spaniel; they were greatly amused that in the picture it was the dog's face which had been painted out to protect his identity. When Alison caught me laughing with them she was furious. Somehow Mrs Byers from the church group got to hear about this and when I met her in the Co-op she launched off into one of her computer rants. She was entirely convinced that if they played too much with computers they would go blind, so they needed lots of exercise to keep their thoughts wholesome. Truly her vast bosoms quivered with indignation.

As the children were getting older, visits from the vicar became more strained, largely thanks to the challenges Ben insisted on posing to Christianity.

'Are you God's best friend?' he asked Mr Bollow.

'We are all his friends.'

'Were you there when he was arrested?'

'Excuse me?'

'Well, on the seventh day he was arrested. Mr Keller who we buy our wine from says God has been performing miracles turning water into wine and it'll put him out of business. And he was allowing people to buy too much cheap booze so he deserved to be arrested. Mr Keller says God can't possibly be his friend. He says God is to blame for people beating each other up and hospitals being really busy with drunk people when they should be looking after people who are really ill.'

'Ah yes, these are most interesting ecclesiastical ideas and I'm so pleased that...'

'And why aren't we fish?' interrupting rudely.

'Ah yes...' eyes swivelling madly, looking for Marianna to save him from this excruciating torture.

'Miss Samuels our geography teacher says that seventy per cent of the earth is water and God must have known this so why didn't he give us gills? And why does God make so many mistakes? Mr Samuels said that he had to kick Satan out of heaven because he was naughty so why did he create Satan? And he says you get rich looking after us, and he made a mistake with Noah too. I saw you putting water on to baby Toby's head but all Noah's friends got drowned.'

'Aaah...'

'And Mr King our history teacher says that the reformation made us all into prostitutes where the church... '

'Protestants!' the wretched vicar hissed, backing in terror away from his nemesis. At the door he turned and dashed wildly down the corridor in a most unecclesiastical manner past a trio of savages eating sticky cakes in the kitchen. "Have a cake Vicar?' grunted one of them, offering a cake held out in a filthy paw which had not had the remotest flirtation with soap for some time; and he was convinced that one of the currants moved. Not even Marianna's charms would bring him back for a while.

* * * * * *

Summer brought the still, invasive heat of windless days and motionless air, the scorched grass in the meadows turning quickly to hay. You could watch buzzards languidly spiralling higher and higher in a cloudless sky, with no escape from the overpowering heat. Even the insects and wildlife would sleep through the midday, with no movement until sunset threatened and shadows appeared and lengthened. Then the world would awake and hunting would begin in the undergrowth. Bees and butterflies, dragonflies transparent with colour and speed, small mammals, were all busy about their urgent routines. The farm awoke, with chickens, ducks and geese all emerging into the cool of the evening, watching for the fox and the rat. And the woodpeckers were drumming, the magpies spying and thieving and the horses and cows trying vainly to lash away their plagues of flies.

In the orchard, the children had hours of fun, but the plum trees in the churchyard were even more tempting. Ben and Trixie would vault the wall into the forbidden grounds, tiptoeing past the graves and the haunted yew tree to the sacred plum tree, which must be stripped of its fruit (though never, under any circumstances, at night). Old Edwin the herdsman, who was even more ancient than Granny, would breathe stories of ghouls he had seen there on stormy and clouded nights, when the gargoyles on the roof would come to life and move soundlessly among the mounds in the graveyard.

Yes, the graveyard was a constant source of fear and excitement to both children and adults. But back on our side of the wall a more tangible danger was presented by the hordes of drunken wasps which feasted on fermenting windfalls. The game was to wade in among them with badminton rackets and smack them into oblivion. If one got lodged in your hair or clothes, the wasp had the last laugh. So there was a constant lookout for newcomers to the village. 'What nice friendly children to make Dominic so welcome!' parents would say, until little Dominic, unused to this robust country game, returned howling, with wasp stings all over his body.

Ben and Trixie quickly became experts. They sought out wasps' nests, put a hosepipe in and flooded the nest until the swarms came out to attack a circle of warrior-children yelling and screaming with joyful spontaneity as the insects dived to the attack and everyone got stung.

And then there was the fun of collecting bags of semi-rotten windfalls, climbing into the laurel bushes and pelting the dogs next door. On one occasion one of Ben's friends targeted Mr Dodds, and the rotten missile splattered against the barn wall just by his head. A most satisfactory result. With a bellow of fury, Mr Dodds charged at the bushes, but all the miscreants were long gone by then.

There followed a furious phone call.

'But it couldn't have been one of us. Maybe it was one of the yobs from the recreation ground?'

'The only yobbos are the ones living right there with you!' shouted Mr Dodds, savagely slamming down the phone.

'What manners! Ben, what do you know about this?'

'James was aiming at me but he missed and nearly hit Mr Dodds'

A muffled snort came from behind the door, and Granny clump-clumped her way into the room wearing her sensible shoes.

'Hah! A likely story' she said, frowning at Ben. Her face was more lined than before her accident and her greyish hair was cut short, largely thanks to Alison's influence. She had now taken to wearing loose-fitting skirts and tops with colourful wild flower patterns, though she did tend to wear them day after day until her daughter managed to persuade her to change in the interests of hygiene.

'We need to start collecting' she said. 'For winter. The forces! Gathering, gathering. They have not gone away. They wait! They *swooop*...! I have made a list. We need henbane, chamomile, evening primrose, valerian, hyssop, eucalyptus... we must work in the fields, gathering all we can. Children, you can help!'

Suddenly Ben wasn't there.

CHAPTER SIXTEEN

'This is SO boring' grumbled Trixie almost apologising as both children had invited some friends from school to help. The day of Granny's picnic had arrived and she had completed her list of plants, flowers and bush clippings for the rest of us to collect.

'Now, coltsfoot, valerian and yellow gentian' she began. 'They grow in the fields. She made a dramatic sweeping gesture with one arm. It was hardly helpful in working out exactly which fields she wanted us to search, let alone whereabouts within them. 'Angelica, mountain ash, oak and yew are all found in the forest and near the water. For protection!' She looked accusingly at Alison. 'Your Rescue Remedy. Clematis, cherry, rockrose, star of Bethlehem, so pretty. Bunches of clover we need too. The Trinity, you see!'

'These plants go back centuries, much older than Christ' put in Vadoma.

'Florika, you must get coral. We need this, you see, against lightning.' She punched her chest and looked to the heavens. 'In the old days they thought coral was a plant. And we need nettles, lots and lots of nettles, to burn in the house, they stop lightning in the winter storms. And lots of juniper, bay branches. Bunches of bracken. They give protection during storms. They keep witches and ghosts away.'

'Oh Granny, we're never going to find all those' protested Trixie.

'It does sound a bit ambitious' put in Alison.

'Nonsense! Lots of these herbs already grow right here in the garden. You know what they all look like. Do they teach you nothing at school?'

The summer garden was always beautiful, in a tangled sort of way. The forest around it was a tapestry of sun-warmed translucent glass which filtered through the trees, motes of dust and midges floating in the sun beams. The grassy areas were awash with colour, wild flowers dominated by statuesque ox eye daisies which colonised the rougher banks in their thousands. In the afternoon the golden light would caress the meadow and dragonflies and dreamy butterflies would hover over the pond in a salute to millions of generations of their predecessors. The still water, with shade-softened banks where horses quietly flicked and snoozed until dusk, would offer its coolness, and the growing shadows would be dominated by the deep red of the sinking sun on the western horizon. Then the quiet evening would abruptly become crowded with insect, bird and water life in a spontaneous explosion of activity, the tranquillity and heat shattering in a frantic last-minute rush to feed before darkness, when swooping owls and other nocturnal dangers would hold sway.

There was the same sort of peace over the estuary, where

dew-damp coated the grass and leaves and placed crystal drops on to the delicate lacework of spider's webs. The rickety wooden jetty which stretched over the shallows gave shade and a vantage point to stare down into the mud of the river, to observe secretly the many lives beneath.

Alison had driven Granny down there early, for we knew her mother would not be able to stay very long; her stamina faded quickly. Soon afterwards the rest arrived, between them lugging a vast hamper, chairs, tables, rugs and a complete set of noise and bedlam. Trixie had brought her best friend, a German exchange student called Dagmar, who had old-fashioned manners. At least, she did until she came to us. On her return her parents will find that they have swapped their model of grace and deportment for a prime example of modern Gothic chic. They will be pleased.

A suitable base camp was set up in a grassy glade and the children were sent off to hunt for plants. Everyone was allocated a list to find and despatched in an appropriate direction. In reality all the boys wanted to do was to throw stones at the ducks, while the girls set off in pursuit of the horses, which were far too alert to let them anywhere near and moved smartly off to positions from which they could watch the proceedings in safety.

While Granny directed, Vadoma supervised and the children hunted, Marianna and Steve, having been spared such duties, began to sort out the picnic. Steve seemed to be Marianna's constant companion now, though as far as we could tell she was allowing no actual contact. It seemed she was fascinated and repelled by him in equal measure.

'She too good for that man' Vadoma told us. 'She get much better man if she want, but she scared to leave village. He got nice eyes, but creepy or what!'

No sooner had Steve and Marianna opened the first tins and boxes than the wasps, flies, ants and other creepy-crawlies appeared unannounced and certainly uninvited, like those gatecrashers one reads about who learn of a party through facebook and end up trashing both the party and the house. One wonders if our guests are the same ones, or relatives, of those unhoused when the old sofa in the study was re-upholstered. This had hidden quietly in state for over fifty years in a largely unexplored corner where it had erected a defensive barrier of boxes, books and sundry heavy items in a laager of protection. Looking carefully it could be seen snuggly relaxing having escaped the horror of countless teenage bottoms, bogey encrusted fingers and other unspeakable joys. But such is the fate of sofakind that this blissful tranquillity could not last. It was dragged out for inspection and then publicly stripped. The children were sworn to secrecy because if Mrs Dodds or the vicar heard about this truly shocking act of public indecency they would summon the police with tales of immorality involving a strange girl called Sophy. Mrs Dodds would retire in shock, while the vicar would want to find out who the girl is and indeed witness such depravity for himself. Dirty old goat. He would get a surprise; especially when given a whip to 'thrash the dust out', one of those exciting euphemisms which are more usually associated with basements in Bayswater.

Eventually the children returned, summoned by hunger and thirst and laden down, despite childish distractions, with armfuls of leaves, branches, flowers and whole plants, which were all stuffed in an orgy of disorganisation into the car. They then descended on to the beautifully set out picnic with nimble fingers which quickly picked out the ants from the sandwiches with appropriate exclamations of horror (these are the same children who happily watch guests tucking into scones with liberal helpings of currants), the pork pies, the scotch eggs where the eggs pop out and roll away to be rescued promptly before hordes of giant dung beetles arrive to carry off these albino monsters in a grotesque ritual of somersaults, and the cakes; and more insects kept arriving. But even greater disgust was displayed towards various unidentified messes in plastic pots prepared by Vadoma, which had a definite Rumanian tang to them.

Dagmar seemed to know all about these, which we felt was suspicious. She fitted in surprisingly well, though she was a bit sniffy about our car, which was not only not German (unlike the previous one) but to be fair, had quickly come to look like a miniature landfill site.

As the afternoon rolled on towards dusk the children started drifting back towards the house, with many last-minute herbal contributions being stuffed into the back of the car for Granny to sort later. She had left some time before, ostensibly to prepare room for her newcomers. Steve had announced that he was going off exploring.

Marianna sat alone absorbing the peace and quiet of the glade, relieved that the children had scattered and left her in peace. She kicked off her shoes and wriggled her toes in the grass, throwing her head back to let the last of the late afternoon sun warm her throat. But even as she did so she noticed that the sky had turned an odd colour. The blue had changed to a leaden grey, streaked with fire. And the birds had stopped singing. The wood seemed suddenly to have been struck dumb. It was time to go.

'Why is it that what fits into the hamper to get here, won't fit in again!' she muttered to herself, busily ramming cups, plates and knives back into the hamper. 'There is not more but less. This I do not understand!' she complained, to no one in particular. But she was feeling distinctly uneasy.

Then she felt the hairs on the back of her neck stiffen. She knew without doubt that she was being watched from the woodlands. She swung around; nothing. She hadn't had a premonition like this since that intensely private moment in the catacombs, but this was different. Though the late afternoon sun was warm and there was no wind, a sudden coldness surrounded her. It was not a physical sensation of chill, but rather a chilling of the mind, a corrosive and creeping fear as those unseen eyes raked her body.

'Steve! Steve! she called. 'Where are you? We must go, it's cold!'

She heard a rustle and turned to see Steve emerge from the bushes. 'Why? It's nice here. Peace and quiet, nothing wrong with that' he said.

'Nothing, I just want to go home!' She spoke more sharply than she had intended. She did not want to transmit her fear to whatever was watching, but she still half expected something to attack from the rear as they tidied up the remains of the picnic and carried it to the car. Once inside, she leaned forward with her head against the steering wheel, conscious that she was trembling like a tightly-wound spring.

'You OK? Shall I drive?' suggested Steve, appearing to notice for the first time that something had happened to Marianna. He knew he was not the most sensitive person but even he could see, or sense, that changes were happening again, not only to her but to the village community. It seemed to be getting more pronounced as the coldness of autumn nights began to warn of winter.

'No, no, I'll be OK' she said, determined to pull herself together. She turned the key and drove rather too quickly up the lane towards the village.

'Come on, we must unload and find Granny. We'll see where she wants all this stuff.'

They soon found her. The cellar door was open and from the depths of Hades rose a man's voice – unintelligible, stumbling words with all manner of windy accompaniment.

'Granny must have an orchestra down there' said Trixie to Dagmar, who had just arrived back at the house and was completely unprepared for yet another Anglo-Saxon surprise.

Staring down into the darkness, past the rising strangulation of alcoholic fumes, the raw slurring of voices, the crash of glass with vulgar and aggressive comments, the explosion of rampant elderflower wine bottles was yet another tranquil day below stairs. We found the vicar administering to Granny while simultaneously embracing the evils of alcohol. Granny, always with a ready welcome for a drinking buddy, was slouched in the corner muttering something about Bing Crosby. She couldn't stand. We shooed the vicar upstairs, and he tripped over the mat at the top, bounced once and cannoned (particularly appropriate) off two walls before staggering erratically through the door. He must have another meeting to go to, pointed out Trixie, who was clinging onto Dagmar, both of them practically collapsing with helpless laughter.

This was followed by the most alarming clattering and screeching as he cycled off with two flat tyres, the sharp metal rims grinding a deep groove into the soft tarmac strip where the council had yet again dug the road up. Curses floated in the air in the general direction of the council estate where the culprits lurked, while his legs worked like fat little pistons. More seriously, explanations were required later when old Lady Sloane upended herself against the vicarage gate because in her efforts to avoid the wobbling vicar, her wheelchair had got stuck in a mysterious new rut. It took on a life of its own, careering towards the church giving her Ladyship a nasty turn as she thought she had received The Summons and her time had come. But no angels or heavenly choirs welcomed her into the ecclesiastical shrubbery although being tipped head first allowed her legs to flash a rude sign at those bad mannered enough to stare. She was eventually helped out of her predicament by Mrs Vicar doing her best Eeyore impression about the hopelessness of life; how there's no respect for the old; the politicians are clearly to blame for everything.

The story caused great mirth in the Green Man. Lady Sloane had few friends in the village, thanks to her habit of waiting in the Co-op queue and loudly complaining that the queues wouldn't be there if the hoi polloi from the estate were restricted to certain shopping hours. Not being content with this, she then caused mayhem in a recent parish council meeting by suggesting that council tax could be reduced if the council saved electricity by turning off the catseyes after 10 o'clock. Everybody just looked at each other in astonishment, and then spontaneous clapping broke out. Lady Sloane, visibly moved, was overwhelmed that such a common sense suggestion should have been received with such accolade. Privately she was firmly resolved to continue serving on as many committees as possible; it seemed her clear thinking was much needed; indeed appreciated.

As we started to retrieve Granny from the cellar, there came a further shock. We were met by a scene of chaos which seemed beyond even Granny's capabilities. Empty bottles lay in satiated abandonment over the floor and were perched precariously on shelves, on wooden cases, and on some large decorative barrels I had bought from the wine merchant....and on which the next day he had no memory of and was convinced that he'd been robbed. There was a stink of strong tobacco, but no sign of smoke.

'Granny, what on earth has been happening here?' asked Alison, shocked at the scenes of unbridled debauchery. We had seen no evidence of visitors, either coming or going. There were no cars outside, no coats, no hints of strangers.

'Oh, they were all here when I arrived. Didn't you invite them? Then the Vicar dropped in too. Must have been twenty of us. Some very rough types. Rude songs!' She rolled her eyes; a huge smile splitting her face. 'But when you arrived they all left' she finished crossly.

'What do you mean they left? We didn't see anybody!' I was completely mystified.

'Oh no, you wouldn't have. They went that way.' She pointed vaguely at the brick wall at the far end of the cellar.

Alison and I looked at each other. Clearly, Granny really was dementing. I stepped over to the far wall and looked for some evidence of a way through, just in case there was some access we had missed in the gloom of the poor lighting. But the red brick wall was old and solid with the mortar starting to flake and fall away from between the bricks. There were piles of dust, mortar and brick debris in long-undisturbed heaps, but there was no sign of any kind of door. She must be imagining the whole thing. Clearly she was becoming even more crazy than we thought.

'Even those two couldn't have drunk all this by themselves' Alison said. Both our minds were searching for some kind of rational explanation. In vain.

CHAPTER SEVENTEEN

The next day it was as if a switch had been thrown. Suddenly summer had ended, replaced overnight by winter. The arrival of a bitter easterly plunged the house and us into a gloomy greyness. A powdering of premature frost had descended quietly over the land. The leaves, yellow, gold, red and brown, were merging soundlessly into spellbinding colours. The birds were taken by surprise, the residents buckling down to the rigours of winter while the dilettantes were leaving in vast curves and patterns against the cold blue sky, always moving, moving southwards. The hens and ducks, isolated from nature by centuries of domestication, barely noticed.

The pigeons and squirrels sought warm nooks in the church roof to escape from the sharp east wind. The mice were on the move again, finding their way to sanctuary in the house. It had survived another summer, although there were sterner tests to come. It certainly gave a natural welcome to the invading wildlife, because Granny had festooned every corner, every shelf and mantelpiece with vegetation. It was as if the plants, sensing a retreat from the rigours of winter, had moved into the house to provide a warmer welcome for other refugees.

In every room was a bunch of angelica. 'The flowers keep witches away and the aniseed keeps the rooms fresh' Granny pointed out. Alison looked on, not entirely convinced, especially when she stood under one bunch and a large and hairy spider alighted on her right shoulder with a cheerful 'here I am' twinkle in its eyes. But it quickly saw the look of horror on Alison's face so its fat fuzzy legs galvanised into action and it scuttled back up its lifeline, to recover in hiding. Leaving both in shock.

There were sprigs of rowan everywhere, their long multi-leaved stems tightly bunched with their glowing sprays of red berries. Down the corridors stood a row of two-foot-high vases carrying branches of oak, yew and bay sticking out, waiting to snag any loose-fitting sweaters, or even worse, to brush gently against any passers-by on a dark night during one of the repeated power cuts. Many visitors had fled to their rooms overcome with shock, having been caressed in the dark by an unseen presence in an empty corridor, and had appeared at breakfast the next morning with alarming tales of nocturnal experiences. 'Not in front of the children!' Granny would interrupt quickly, quite misunderstanding the direction the conversation was going. And everywhere small bags of 'Granny's Ghosts' Potpourri' were placed, hidden or hung, strange mixtures of mugwort, yarrow, rosemary, clover, dill and countless other mysterious and secret fusions. And there were tortured roots of yellow herb bennet hanging next to other roots making some rooms look like a deli with swarms of pregnant salamis mutating soundlessly from the beams.

It was Vadoma's task to check these weekly to keep their protective strength up. 'We must do this!' Granny would say. 'I feel the earth stirring, there are forces, beware the forces of winter!' And Vadoma would nod in agreement.

'What are we going to do with her?' I asked Alison. She just shrugged helplessly.

The old house was already starting to complain; groaning, swearing and creaking as joints began to contract in the cold. Windows suddenly developed leaks as the glass contracted faster than the frames. The frames were anchored and supported by thick stone walls, with only mildew and rot to challenge their cosy symbiosis; the panes had no such comfort. Marianna had to scour the charity shops for buckets and large containers which would be placed in emergency spots for quick deployment when the leaking began. The long icy passageways, threadbare Persian rugs, pictures of forgotten wars, ancestors hanging drunkenly from the picture rails crashing to the floor with a monotonous regularity as the string breaks, usually at three in the morning all contributed to a cold and hostile environment.

Floorboards creaked and the wind whistled mournfully through the window frames with a menacing consistency, the dull moaning sound persuading many weekend guests to cut their visits short. The ancient coat of armour at the top of the stairs projected an aura of fear, particularly when it seemed to tremble in response to the gusts. Desperate guests would sidle past fearfully in the dark on the way to the loo and firmly lock the door. Ben's favourite trick was to turn the landing lights out when they tried to make the return journey.

One of the most worrying disturbances occurred after some friends of Alison's from London, Piers and Wendy Howarth and their three daughters, had arrived for a weekend visit on a cold and storm-tossed Friday night.

'Doesn't it ever stop raining in this country?' asked Vadoma irritably while she was busily 'creating' in the kitchen. The house was battened down, all windows were securely locked with curtains drawn and the outer doors were bolted to stop them rattling and wheezing in the gusts of wind which attacked them with a vengeful fury. It was like a personal anger which hurled a driving muscular energy to try to force entry. Meanwhile inside, the kitchen emanated warmth and security, the smells of cooking creating a shelter from the vigorous wildness just inches away.

'I bet they're going to be late, having to drive through this' said Alison. 'I hope there are no trees down.'

'What are the odds?' Granny perked up.

'Oh Granny, it's just an expression. I must stop saying that.' She looked crossly at Granny, who managed to look not a bit contrite.

As she spoke there was the crunch of tyres on gravel outside, and headlights lit up the front rooms, throwing a ghostly light through the curtains.

Then all hell broke loose. The dogs were going frantic at the front door with their bedlam of barking and scrabbling competing with the uproar of Ben and Trixie yelling at them to stop it. The sheer scale of the chaos brought Granny out to add her particular brand of confusion, but she had to be sidelined to keep her safe from the seething mass of animals and people. Trying to sideline Granny caused even more raucous tumult.

'Where did those bloody animals come from?' she bawled in a most vulgar fashion. She meant the dogs, presumably.

'They live here, Granny' I pointed out, hauling on Rufus' collar. Meanwhile Alison had opened the front door upon the miserable sight of two adults and three girls standing soaked in the downpour while trying to extract their suitcases and bags from a muddy and shabby-looking Range Rover, purchased brand new the previous week and already looking too ashamed to be seen in Chelsea.

'Come in, come in!' urged Alison. 'Ben, control those bloody dogs!' They were whipping themselves into a frenzy. Eventually - it seemed like ages but in reality was only a minute or two - they were dragged into the kitchen and the door firmly closed. But this seemed only to increase their hysteria.

'Granny, you remember Piers?' Alison shouted.

'Of course I do, and I'm not deaf so you don't need to shout!' she snapped back crossly. 'But he doesn't live here.'

'No Granny, this is Piers.'

'Oh no dear, Piers lives in London' she replied. 'And who is this? Why is his hair all slicked back? Has he been swimming? You're lucky to find us here you know, we're moving soon.'

'No Granny, you've moved... look, come and have a gin' I said, trying to edge her away to wherever she could do the least amount of damage.

'Yes, about time too' she said. 'Now look, it's getting dark and we still haven't had lunch.' The children were all in fits of giggles by this stage, and we could see Piers and Wendy silently praying that the rest of the weekend would be a little less riotous.

While the Howarths stood drying themselves off in the hall, Trixie and the girls swarmed up the stairs to the large bedroom at the end of the corridor which they were all going to share for the weekend. The noise of giggling and shrieking fell off as they reached the landing. Alison showed Piers and Wendy to their room while Ben and I found sanctuary with the dogs and Granny in the kitchen.

'I still don't know who those people are' complained Granny in a slightly cantankerous tone, 'is Alison running a hotel here?'

The evening meal was the usual cacophony, but was saved by superb cooking. I could see Alison was elated at having a houseful of guests and seeing the family revelling in their companionship. Once the initial chaos had subsided the Howarths proved to be appreciative and convivial guests, and the tension soon relaxed.

* * * * * *

Outside the house, other things were stirring besides the

weather. The intensity of the storm seemed to be growing and as the evening drew on there was no sign of it abating. There was something sinister in that it seemed to hover over the village; there was no movement away, which surely would have been normal.

Later in the evening, I peered through the curtains to see that the village was bathed in an eerie light which fluctuated in intensity as huge black clouds galloped and writhed over the treetops. One second the moon was swathed and a deep darkness plunged over the land, and the next the mantle had split asunder to allow through a sharp white clarity. But it brought with it a coldness and menace. And in the darkness angry shapes hurled blankets of rain towards earth and the wildness of the night was jolted by crashes of thunder while bayonets of zigzag lightning thrust vigorously into the nearby woodlands as if on a personal vendetta to seek and destroy the old oak tree and the mystical creatures which it protected. The occasional blinding flash of sheet lightning would illuminate the earth as if all the demons in the universe had congregated their powers, bringing a momentary stillness and a fearful shroud of evil.

Then, without warning, the lights started flickering and dimming and then went out completely. An instant and chilling silence filled the house. All we could hear was the scrabbling and whining of the dogs.

Alison, always ready for any emergency, produced candles, which we stood up in saucers. Together with the open fire, they gave off an aura which in any other circumstances would have infused the room with security, even romance. But any such thoughts were far away. The dogs cringed, fur bristling, ears sharply forward. Their bright eyes were watching the chimney and the smoke which was continuing to rise up from the fire. But the smoke was no longer white; it had acquired a strange blackness which now moved more urgently upwards.

In the stillness the storm suddenly made itself felt within the house. The thunder sounded louder while the wind bullied and shook the windows and doors as if it was determined to tear them apart. Rain steadily pattered against the glass, punctuated by the abrupt machine-gun attack of what sounded like hailstones. The old timbers started again to creak and contract as the house shuddered, making doors fidget and stretch within their frames. It was as if the full might of the storm had decided to focus itself upon the house.

Then came a huge crash, and the cellar door flew open to smash against the wall with such violence that it bounced back again on to the latch. I quickly secured the door and removed the key, as I had done so many times before.

'The wind is angry' said Vadoma, who was sitting reading by the fire.

'God knows how the kids can sleep through this' I muttered to Alison.

By now it was close to midnight. Armed with candles, we all trooped upstairs. The dogs were making it clear that they did not want to be left alone in their baskets in the kitchen.

Finally, relative quiet descended on the house, and the clocks ticked on into the night. Outside, the storm raged.

CHAPTER EIGHTEEN

I woke up suddenly. The green glow of the bedside clock showed 3.12 am; Alison was sleeping quietly. I lay there with my mind racing, knowing that something had disturbed me, but unable to think what.

I lay very still and listened for a moment. The storm had calmed to a gentle patter of rain against the window, and the wind was sighing in the background as it whispered around the house. It all seemed so calm now, as if the recent test of strength had been resolved and the house and the wild forces outside had realigned themselves into a comfortable alliance.

It had not been the weather which had awoken me – but what?

Again I had that feeling of not being alone, of being watched by something or someone unfamiliar. I sensed a brooding menace lurking somewhere close. A soft moon was now shining through the curtains, leaving shadows and unlit corners which held pools of impenetrable darkness.

I sat up and looked around. I tried the lights, but of course they still weren't working. Then, as I looked carefully at the faint outline of the cupboard, I thought I saw a shadowy movement in my peripheral vision, by the door to the landing. Something moved, a grey blur which detached itself from the corner of the room and whisked out of the door. It was a shape, formless yet real. There was no sound, no footsteps on the bare boards, no rustle of clothing. But it left behind a bitter coldness which transcended the normal winter chill, an oppressive dampness which was unusual even for this house. And there came with it something else I had sensed before; a ghastly smell of putrescence and decay.

My tension must have woken Alison, who now sat up.

'What's happened? What are you doing?' she asked in a bleary voice. 'It's so cold! Don't say the heating's gone off.'

'I don't know, but I thought I saw something moving, a shadow, I don't know what it was. I'll go and check the children.' I got out of bed and quickly wrapped my towelling dressing gown around me. 'I'll have a look at the boiler.'

Then we both heard the sound of footsteps from above.

'Granny!' I said. 'Wouldn't you just know it. Surely she's not messing with her plants at this time of the morning?'

'It's not Granny' said Alison, now wide awake. 'There's more than one person up there, surely she hasn't got Vadoma with her? I'll come with you.' She swung her legs out of the bed and grabbed her thin nightgown.

'My God it's cold. What on earth is that smell?'

'I don't know. Maybe the drains have frozen up, or maybe they're being overwhelmed. We do have a house full. But it's not really that sort of smell. More like a cat or a squirrel or something has died in the loft space.'

'That could be it. Remember last summer when we found all those dead crows up the chimney?'

Alison shuddered. An investigation of the chimney had produced a disgusting avalanche of corvid bodies, skeletons, beaks and twisted feet. With visions of hairy Dickensian soot-stained rascals, we had asked the local sweep to pay a visit, and were relieved to find that he shoved a steel brush and a suction device up the chimney instead of a small boy. The pump made an efficient job of sucking out all the corpses and feathers, leaving only a lingering pong which permeated the downstairs for some days; it was a malevolent whiff for which Granny got the blame. You could see Mr Bollow sniffing the air, wondering who we had buried under the floorboards and performing a surreptitious headcount to see if anyone was missing. He took a dim view of unauthorised burials, and focused especially on the log basket where the contorted branches flirted with images of human limbs.

We laughed together at that, the cold and the reason for our being awake temporarily forgotten. This was the strength of our relationship. We could recall events in the most unlikely places and inappropriate times and laugh together.

But this time our reminiscences were interrupted by a shrill scream from the girls' bedroom.

'I'll go, get some candles!' I yelled at Alison. I could hear the dogs going berserk in the kitchen, barking and scrabbling at the door to get into the corridor, or perhaps just to get out of the kitchen, where they had been sleeping more or less contentedly every night for months.

I ran quickly out of the door and into the corridor, only to find that the passageway was blocked by the oak settle, which had somehow been moved from its position against the wall and now stood diagonally across the landing. Other doors were opening now. Piers and Wendy were trying to squeeze past a large white porcelain jar containing a stack of Granny's plants, which was blocking their door. Vadoma and Marianna both had to scramble past piles of chairs which had been stacked outside their rooms.

'What's happening?' asked Wendy, looking very tousled and confused.

'I don't know. Who put these here?' I asked 'Let's just check the children.'

We pushed our way past all the obstacles and headed for the girls' room. Alison caught us up with a supply of candles, which we lit before heading into their room.

All the children were clustered around Trixie's bed. That dreadful smell of decay was back, and now it was overpowering.

We entered to see Trixie sitting up in bed, looking as if she was in a trance. She was staring with large, unblinking eyes at the window. The curtains were closed, but faint moonlight shone through the thin material to bathe the room in a chilly glow. The flickering candles gave off a subdued light which emphasised writhing shadows in the corners where the glow couldn't reach. The icy cold was even worse in this room than it had been in ours.

'Trixie! Are you OK? What's happened?' Alison asked in a tone of voice which had an uncharacteristic sharpness. Trixie just stared, unmoving, at the window. Then her eyes slowly swivelled around to look at us all crowded around her, and life returned. Her lips started to quiver and she threw herself into Alison's arms.

'He was here, standing by my bed looking at me!' she sobbed, the words tumbling out, barely articulate.

'Who was here darling, tell me?' Alison said very quietly, her whole attention focused on our shocked daughter. She held her tight and stroked her hair as if she was calming a frightened animal.

'I couldn't see his face. It was just his shadow against the window. He had a big round hat on and he had a cloak on and he was bending over my bed. His hands were coming close to my face, they were like skeleton fingers, all long and sharp and his mouth was black, it was horrible. He really stank! He went away when I screamed.'

'Well, you're safe now. Did anyone else see anything? Are the rest of you OK?' There was a general shrugging of shoulders and shaking of heads. 'It must have just been a very bad dream' offered Piers in explanation, and an attempt to comfort.

The sound of bedlam was still coming from the kitchen. 'Ben, Piers, come on we'll go down and sort out the dogs. We can't do any more here' I said to Alison, who nodded her agreement.

'Does anyone know who put all these things in the passageway?' I asked the gathering.

'It's the poltergeist' Ben said. 'I told you I saw one.'

'No, that was Trixie dressed up' I laughed.

I went out on to the landing, looking at the chaos. Once again I felt that momentary sensation of being watched. I turned to walk towards the stairs and then, as I passed the big gilded mirror at the top of the stairs, I caught a glimpse in it, just for a moment, of a face behind me. It was like a shadow shimmering in the candlelight and was vaguely familiar; a strong, man's face with a square chiselled jaw, piercing grey eyes under hooded brows which gave an air of concealment under a large brimmed hat. He left a rapier-like penetration of foulness within my mind; an instant to see, a lifetime to remember.

Instinctively I looked over my shoulder to see who was behind me. The landing was empty.

I looked back at the mirror, and as I did so it began to shake. Then with a huge crash it fell on to the top stair and cartwheeled down to the hall below, the glass cascading everywhere in a pagan premonition of bad luck.

'What the...? shouted Piers, rushing out to see what the noise was. We all stood there, numb with surprise, looking at the mess.

'Kids, don't even think of going down there till we've cleared it up!' said Alison.

'Leave it to me' said the subdued voice of Vadoma from behind me. She had an aura of calm acceptance, as if somehow she had expected these events to happen.

'I'll do it' she whispered. She was looking at me mysteriously.

'OK, let's go down to the kitchen.' The noise was, if anything, getting worse. But I couldn't help noticing Vadoma and Ben exchange a wink. They seemed to know something I did not.

I hurriedly pulled some clothes on, and Vadoma put on her dressing gown and slippers. While Alison, Wendy and Marianna saw to the girls, we walked very gingerly down the stairs towards the darkness of the ground floor, using our candles to light a path and hugging the edges to avoid the shards of glass. Some of the fragments had landed point uppermost, almost as if they had been positioned there deliberately to pierce unwary feet. Still we could feel that dreadful coldness penetrating everything.

As we went down the corridor to the kitchen the candles threw out an unearthly panorama of shapes and spectres which coiled and twisted against the walls. The smell of decay hung so heavily as to be almost visible.

We opened the kitchen door and crowded in, to meet a scene of devastation. Before us lay a landscape of destruction. Broken crockery, cutlery, glass, pots and pans were jumbled up in an orgy of havoc all over the floor. Rufus was standing in the far corner facing the cellar door, the hair along his back standing on end in fear. Behind him cowered Muffin, whimpering softly. The cellar door stood slightly ajar.

I reached for my heavy torch and gave a smaller one to Vadoma. 'Ben, try and calm the dogs. Piers, could you close the window?' It had certainly not been open the previous evening.

'Something must have got in to cause all this damage. Perhaps they were chasing a badger or something' offered Piers as he carefully picked his way through the debris. He is, of course, not a countryman. Meanwhile I was looking at the cellar door. The key was on the floor, as if it had been casually dropped there. The dark of the steps leading down seemed almost to be a challenge, with a gloom so intense that it had a physical presence.

'Ben, bring the dogs' I said. Both animals seemed more confident with us in the room, but on approaching the top of the stairs they again started the enraged barking. They were both glaring downwards with wild eyes, legs braced aggressively. I pushed past them and started down.

'Ben, stay up here and tell your mother where we are!' I shouted up at him as Piers and I descended into the blackness. As we moved down the steps, they gave off a sinister creaking sound which almost obscured the scratching and scuffing coming from the depths. The noises seemed to be amplified by the curved roof of the cellar and bounced back and forth as if there was a pack of rats scrabbling at the very foundations of the house. The twisting, macabre dancing of the candle-shadows added a particular horror of their own.

'Come on you two!' I shouted up at the dogs when we'd got to the bottom of the stairs. Piers was lighting more candles and placing them on the boxes and barrels which sprawled over the floor. By their light we saw more devastation, with empty bottles, broken crates and upturned chairs, as if an unruly crowd had left in a hurry. The dogs were strangely quiet now, uncertain as to what was expected of them. They headed through the chaos to the wall at the far end of the cellar, the same spot Granny had indicated some months before. They sat staring at the wall with ears pointed and heads on one side, straining to listen.

'What do you think they've found?' asked Piers. We went to look. There didn't seem to be any changes since the last time I'd examined it. We tapped the wall to find that the bricks were firm, although the piles of mortar on the floor at the base of the wall seemed to have grown a little.

'Nothing here' I said. 'Let's go back upstairs. We can clear this up later.'

We found the family in the kitchen, Alison and Wendy were making mugs of tea on the gas stove, using an old-fashioned kettle which had last seen service in Victorian times. Vadoma and Marianna were sweeping up the mess on the floor. In a surprisingly short space of time all was back to normal.

Then Alison suddenly turned round.

'Where's Granny?' she asked. We all looked at each other.

'I'll check on her' Vadoma offered.

'OK, I will go with you' I said. Walking up the stairs I saw that Vadoma had done a good job; there were no signs of glass. The cold had gone and the foul smell was much less obvious. I wondered if one of the children had opened the window to let the smell out.

'Were you up there earlier?' I asked Vadoma. 'Alison and I heard footsteps in the attic. We thought you might have been helping Granny.'

'What, three o'clock in morning? Not me!' She shrugged her shoulders.

'You didn't seem all that surprised. I just wondered, you know, with your culture and so on – do you think we have some sort of ghost that moved all the stuff around? A poltergeist?'

She frowned in thought. 'The poltergeist, usually, he is associated with children. He is found in houses close to water. When there are great storms the rivers start to flood. This brings pressure on the land to contain the water, and this pressure somehow releases these poltergeist spirits. They are not ghosts, you know, not spirits from the dead. They are a kind of energy which is generated by children when it is stormy. Here we have many children, and much water.'

I just looked at her. 'I don't know what to believe' I said. 'I'm completely stumped.'

When we got to the attic there was no sign of any disturbance. Vadoma gently eased open Granny's bedroom door and we found her innocently asleep in her favourite dusty old armchair next to the window. An open book was on her lap. Presumably she had dozed off when the lights had gone out.

'Granny is protected up here by all her plants and spells' Vadoma whispered, very seriously. But to my eyes she looked vulnerable and slightly ghost-like as she sat in a shaft of blue moonlight which had trespassed through the window and created a link to the wild sky and the heavens outside. There was a sense of infinite time and distance towards the stars which winked and hid behind the tattered strips of cloud which were darting past the moon giving a mottled light which had a cold but inviting allure. Sleeping there she gave off an aura of unspoken affinity with this ageless beauty; the glimmering constellations of Andromeda and further to the right the stars which anchored Ursa Major, an enduring witness to history. This was a peace not to be disturbed.

Turning away, Vadoma shivered as she pointed to a glimmering menace far away on the northern horizon. 'That is Algol' she whispered. 'It gleams and pulses as it spreads fear and evil. This is the most accursed of all those watching from the heavens, the spirits of the homeless dead'. Her awe-struck eyes looked vast in the darkness.

By the time we had returned to the kitchen we found everybody else going back to their rooms.

'Sleep tight' called Alison. 'We have an early start tomorrow. 'Weather permitting, we'll be walking to the prehistoric fort up on the moors.'

'How's Trix?' I asked her.

'She seems to be OK now' she said. 'I hope she gets back to sleep.'

But as she mentioned the fort, almost on cue, a low grumble of thunder sounded a gentle 'memento mori' from that direction.

CHAPTER NINETEEN

The next day dawned clear, but a bitter wind had now begun to infiltrate every nook and cranny of the house. It sneaked under the doors and even found ways through the loose brickwork of the walls and roof. It was not to be denied entrance by the mere closing of doors and windows, and it added a coldness and moisture to all the corridors and rooms. Outside, fast-moving clouds were hurrying across a fresh blue sky, bringing boisterous gusts and squalls to remind us of the storms which had raged all night over the village. Looking past the church, the woodland trees were brandishing their nakedness towards the sky in a mistral of activity, while the evergreens seemed to be closing ranks around the grey walls in a protective mantle. The church itself stood unchanging in a turbulent world.

Breakfast was a late and subdued 'help yourself' affair as people straggled downstairs in ones and twos, exhausted before the day had even started. The aroma of brewing coffee and the glow of the lights, now functioning again, soon perked everyone up and the events of the night were quickly forgotten.

'Come on, wrap up warm' I told the gathering. 'We're walking up the hill to the moors to see the hill fort. Then lunch at the Green Man. Granny will be meeting us there, but we've told her not to arrive too early. We don't want her falling over before we get there.'

'Steve's coming with us' added Alison. She turned to Piers and Wendy. 'He's our local historian. There isn't much he doesn't know about this area. Marianna has gone to get him.'

We started off in a noisy gaggle, skirting the church on the south side, mainly to avoid upsetting the dogs. The wind, revelling in winter, whipped a freshness and a wet pungent earthiness around us and lashed the old stones as we passed. The countryside had its own rugged brand of winter beauty, so different from the softness and warmth of spring and summer. The paths to the woodlands were still mired in puddles and mud, a primitive reminder of our antecedents in the pre-concrete world. For those who could see, there was still an abundance of hidden wildlife to observe.

We entered the woodlands to find the wind replaced by a welcome and soothing stillness. The trees gave us some temporary respite from the destructive assaults of the gale, still whistling down the valleys and over the moors and seeking out every weakness in its path. But today there was a new feeling, because at ground level we felt an eerie quietness. There was none of the usual background noise of wildlife; no birds sang, no squirrels scampered, no small animals scurried through the dead leaves.

Steve and Vadoma had clearly noticed the unnatural silence, for they looked worried and were speaking together in quiet tones. It was as if nature was waiting for a great event.

Then we broke through the treeline at the base of the high ground and could see the huge panorama of the moors, dominated by the high hill which was capped by the hill fort.

'But there's nothing to see! I was expecting a ruined castle' complained Piers.

'Oh no, this site's about two thousand years earlier' explained Steve. 'But you see that gap between the ridges in front of us? That's the entrance. When we get through you'll see several more very deep ridges. Some of them would have had wooden stockades on them. Any attacking force had to fight up these steep ditches and banks and then get through the wooden barriers.'

As we walked up the steep entrance slope, great ridges and valleys, ditches and banks opened up on both sides.

'When you think you're at the top, another ditch opens in front of you' Steve pointed out. 'You can sense the desperation of the attackers trying to push on to the next ridge, with the defenders pouring spears and arrows down on them. The yelling, the clash of armour, the shrieks of the wounded, the wailing of the Celtic women. The Celts would have been blowing their horns. Carynxes, they called them. The desperation of the defenders who would have felt trapped in the open space on the crown of the hill. The whole community was in mortal danger.'

'Why would people have wanted to attack them?' asked Wendy.

'They wanted their possessions – food, building materials. Once the walls were breached they would have plundered the place wholesale. They'd have taken slaves, raped the women. They had no mercy.'

Piers and Wendy stood there at the top of the ridge, looking down in awe at the rolling waves of lesser ridges stretching before them down to the moors and woodlands below.

'I had no idea' said Wendy. 'It's an amazing place.'

'Come on, let's walk around the perimeter' I suggested. 'It's only half a mile and the view is even better. The children are running ahead, so they're safe.'

'Now you see the bank all round the fort?' Steve pointed it out as we started walking. 'There would have been a high fenced stockade on top of it as a last defence. And inside on this flat area there would have been probably about a hundred mud and wood huts for living and storing food and weapons. In the very middle would have been the tribal meeting place.'

'So it wouldn't have been used for thousands of years?' asked Piers.

'In fact some of these forts were used relatively recently' said Steve. 'During the Civil War there were further battles here. This was a Royalist stronghold, so the Civil War was especially hard on these people. There was a huge amount of killing and witch hunting which usually ended on the gallows. It's had a very violent past going back thousands of years. Hard to imagine when you look how peaceful it is now.'

Vadoma, who had been listening to all this, suddenly looked up and froze. Some distant memory seemed to have struck her. I saw her give Steve a sharp, accusing glance, and he looked away quickly, as if guilty about something.

We continued to walk around the perimeter, Steve and Marianna taking the lead, absorbing the breathtaking views of the surrounding moors, woodlands and villages. The blustery cold helped us to imagine the struggles everyday life must have involved in centuries gone by.

On the far side, we found ourselves overlooking the estuary; and gasped in shock. What had been a series of small streams, gently intertwining like lover's fingers to meander into larger rivers, was now a maelstrom. The courses of the rivers were marked by fast-moving stretches of turbulence, all converging in a frenetic dash to the sea. The reedbeds, the mudflats, the nesting sites and grazing areas of the estuary had disappeared under a muddy deluge which swept seawards to merge in a murky bleakness with the far horizon. From this height we could see that even the sea itself was stained by the estuarial mud. And there was no sign of the old mill.

Many of the caravans in the gypsy encampment were now partially under water, their roofs a resting place for birds and other evacuees from the flood.

'Oh my God!' I said. 'We must find out if Fonso and his family are all right.'

'I hope Florika's all right' said Trixie in dismay. 'Can she come and live with us if they've been flooded?'

'Maybe. Let's find out what's happened first.'

Suddenly I felt wetness on my cheek; a raindrop. It was the signal for a fresh deluge. We had been too overwhelmed by the view below to notice the change in the sky. Huge bruising clouds were sweeping in from the west like a fleet of galleons in full sail. The sounds and sights of the new meteorological battle were truly intimidating on the open space of the hilltop as the thunder began to roll in, with lightning blazing and darting earthwards in almost a personal attack. We fled down the path towards the shelter of the woods, but it was only a matter of seconds before we were all soaked and very cold.

Then, rolling in from the estuary, came the fog. It welled up from below until it met the clouds above, the two merging in a hungry alliance which precluded all else. We were left to struggle, sightless.

The fresh downpour was but a hint of the Armageddon to come, the rain pounding on our heads and backs and the sheer volume of water on the steep path down to the woods producing a mudslide against which it was barely possible to keep standing.

We all headed downhill as fast as we could, some faster than others. Steve and Marianna rushed on while Piers, Wendy, Alison, Vadoma and I tried to stay with the children. The torrential rain and the deeply clinging mist had reduced visibility to no more than a few yards. I arrived at the bottom of the path shouting to try to marshall the party, but my words were flung back into my face by a vengeful wind which howled around my head and which were drowned by the sheer tumult of the thunder and the crashing of the rain as it punched past the trees and danced on the forest floor, drowning out all attempts at communication. I was soaked to the skin and covered in mud and my ears were ringing from the crashing upheavals which were not only in the heavens, but seemed to be all around us.

I tried to look around for the others - and froze in horror. All around me through the curtains of rain, I could see flying shapes – impossible shapes. Out of the wild and churning fog loomed strange figures; the forms of soldiers, of war-horses, of terrified men and women running for their lives. It was like a dream, except that I had never felt more awake in my life. The apparitions and silhouettes all seemed to be heading down the hill, over the ridges and on towards the woods, a mass movement towards the village. And the wild malevolence of the wind echoed around them as the carynx of old must have done giving a desperate urgency to the clamour.

To my shame, I fled in terror, running deeper and deeper into the safety of the trees. The whispering, the soughing of unseen forces followed me, getting ever closer, ever louder. And the fog came with them, snaking in twists and turns around the trees in a ghastly caress. And above it all the storm clouds advanced as if some omnipotent force was coordinating the tempest.

There was movement in the trees, with strange figures shifting in and out of the fog, and the horror was compounded because now I could see terrible things on the ground; butchered and mangled bodies, cadavers with no heads, heads with no bodies, armless corpses and figures with distorted legs, muscular torsos from which the skin had been stripped, horses with their intestines hanging out and dragging behind them, all gliding soundlessly; men, women, children and animals all flowing in a hideous wave, with some dreadful central purpose.

Between all the ghastliness I kept glimpsing Alison and the children, always out of reach. I ran desperately towards them, shouting in despair, but every time I got close they seemed to vanish. Now I heard phantom yells which I thought were human, but the calls trailed off into spine-chilling howls which could never have come from human lungs or human lips. The tortured branches thrashed in protest.

Then suddenly out of the fog came five bedraggled figures; Piers and Wendy and their girls. Somehow they had managed to stay together. They tried to speak, but the storm was too powerful. I signalled them to follow and keep close. We scrambled, slid and fell down the path through the trees back towards the church. Keeping close now, we trudged through the wet and the mud, following the path, a well-trodden lifeline through the undergrowth. Perhaps because we were now moving in a group, the shadows and the apparitions were no longer with us.

At last the dark walls and tower of the church loomed up above us out of the fog, as the bows of the long-lost *Titanic* must have reared horribly up from the cold, black mud of the ocean floor when its modern-day discoverers finally came up

191

on it after nearly a century in its own black and silent tomb. We were almost home.

Outside the house Rufus and Muffin were shivering and whining by the front door, waiting to be let into the safety and shelter of the house. But what of the others? Where were Alison and the children, Vadoma and Marianna?

'Inside, come on, get warm. For Christ's sake, where are the others?' I muttered, a horrible feeling clutching at my stomach. I opened the door and the dogs charged straight into the kitchen, shaking their soaked fur on to the walls.

But they had barely paused to dry themselves when I saw Rufus snarl and make a beeline once again for the cellar door. Yet again it was open.

'Back to your beds!' I yelled, my patience snapping. I was too cold, too wet and too worried about Alison and the children. I slammed the door to the cellar and locked it.

The Howarths plodded forlornly upstairs to dry off and change their clothes while I stood in an agony of indecision. Should I wait for the others to return, or go and look for them? But that seemed hopeless. I would only get lost again myself.

Just as I had made up my mind that I had no choice but to go out and look for them whatever the consequences, the dogs exploded into a frenzy of barking and cascaded in an avalanche of hair, teeth and nails towards the front door; but this time they were driven not by fear but by joy. The door flew open to reveal the soaking, shivering forms of Alison, Trixie, Ben and Vadoma.

'I really thought we were lost' said Alison, hustling the children inside and slamming the door behind them. 'Right, off upstairs and get changed, now' she instructed them. The children, white-faced and drenched, did not need to be told twice. They plodded upstairs, Trixie sobbing quietly and grasping Ben's hand.

'Did you see the ghosts?' yelled Ben as he was shooed upstairs. Even through his fear he was managing a grin.

'Don't be silly, it was just the wind and the fog' Alison snapped, perhaps too quickly.

'Thank goodness you're back, I didn't know what to do' I said. 'Wait a minute – where's Marianna?'

We stared at each other. 'She must be with Steve' said Alison.

'She was at the far end of the hill when the storm broke' said Vadoma. 'I think he went off to find her.'

'She should be all right' I said. But the look of fear on Vadoma's face told me she did not share my confidence.

'Come on, there's tea brewed in the kitchen' I said. 'We'll just have to wait for them.' I led the way through the lake of water which been created by all the wet clothes.

'My God, why didn't you dry off before coming in here? I suppose you thought I would blame the dogs' Alison said sharply.

Vadoma dragged out the mop and started on the floor. Then the Howarths came down in dry clothes, still white-faced but looking a great deal happier now that we had all been safely counted in.

Except Marianna.

And Granny.

'I bet they're in the Green Man' I suggested. 'I suppose Granny must be there as well. They certainly wouldn't have let her leave in this. Come on, I'll buy the drinks.

CHAPTER TWENTY

I gingerly opened the door to discover that the storm had abated a little and the rain was now falling in no more than normal quantities. Having donned the driest clothing we could find, we all drew our coats around us and cantered the two hundred yards to the Green Man. The road was mercifully free of deep puddles. The grass verges were muddy and waterlogged, but the absence of traffic allowed us to walk on the roadway.

We burst panting into the pub to find half the village seemed to be already there toasting the storm, or more likely their escape from it.

'Ah, you made it!' called Steve from the bar.

'And so did you' I replied.

'Granny's over there' he said, pointing to the end of the bar, where my incorrigible mother-on-law was propping up the corner next to the wall mirror. She was already pleasantly squiffy and in deep conversation with her drinking buddy Matilda. The two of them were chatting as if they had been there all day, which indeed they probably had.

'She's not here' said Vadoma, just back from a quick check around all the corners and alcoves in the pub.

'You're joking. Steve, what happened to Marianna?'

'I thought she came back with you' said Steve.

There was a stunned silence. The hubbub from the bar hushed as the drinkers took in our shocked faces.

'Come on, we have to go and find her' said Alison. 'We can't leave her by herself in the woods. Anything could have happened to her.' As she spoke, the storm returned with a deafening crash of thunder, which seemed to be exactly above the Green Man, and the wind and rain battered afresh against the windows and the roof. 'How do we get a search party out in this weather?' asked Piers.

'I'll call Reggie' said Alison. 'He'll know what to do. At least he knows the area, and he can get more people to help if we need them.'

She rushed to the phone behind the bar. Steve handed her the number before she had a chance to ask him. She spoke for a moment or two, then put the receiver down.

'He's coming now' she said. 'He's bringing Fonso with him.'

It was a large and diverse party which gathered at the Green Man over the next twenty minutes. Word had spread until we soon had a force of some thirty people with us. Reg immediately took charge. I was surprised to see a much more forceful character emerging from the relaxed personality I had seen before.

Reg briefed Fonso and his fellow gypsies to sweep the area

between the church and the estuary and then follow the river through the woods up to the hill fort. 'And leave the pheasants alone' he added pointedly. Farmer Salter looked out of the window, pretending not to understand English. Reg and Alison would take the woodland area from the church up to the moors. We would then all meet at the top. Steve seemed content to stay behind, as he was needed to look after the pub. I went with Fonso's group while Reg led the other.

Quite a challenge now faced us. Marianna could be lost, injured or worse anywhere within a couple of square miles of rushing water and treacherous sodden undergrowth, and it had again turned bitterly cold. No one could last long without proper protection in these conditions. But we had to try.

Within minutes we were once again soaked to the skin. The path down to the estuary was now a treacherous mud-slide presenting the constant threat of broken bones and twisted ankles. Within twenty minutes the worry, the cold and the rain had begun to take their toll and several members of the party had already dropped out to head back for warmth and shelter.

When we broke out of the woodlands on to the banks of the estuary, the scale of our task became obvious. The fog had lifted, to be replaced by a wall of rain. The estuary was completely flooded, presenting us with a raging deluge of brown water. The torrent rushed past the bank we were standing on, carrying an armada of uprooted trees, branches, the detritus of wooden buildings, even the carcasses of dead animals and birds, all being repeatedly sucked down to resurface further down on their rush to the sea.

'Keep back!' shouted Fonso. He could see that the bank was being undermined by the water. Even as we watched, a great slab of earth and grass split off from the bank and fell with a crash into the flood. To be whisked away. The river was still rising and the overflow ditches were full. The land was unable to absorb any more water. The flood would only rise further.

'OK, let's walk in line up the bank towards the hill' suggested Fonso. Happy to follow his leadership, we duly spread out. But the line was pathetically short. By now we had been reduced to a rag-tag of no more than half a dozen people. We started the long and arduous walk up the slippery river bank to the hill fort.

Then about thirty minutes into our search, Esmeralda, who had taken the station nearest the river, pointed out something pink floating towards us, in an eddy under the bank.

I crept carefully forward to look. Even as I peered at it, it was snatched by an unseen current into the murky water and swept away, but not before I had recognised it.

I knew exactly what I had seen. It was Marianna's pink quilted jacket. I felt my stomach draw itself into a knot of fear.

'Oh my God!' said Vadoma. 'Oh God, please say she is OK!'

'She may have just lost it' I said. But my suggestion sounded pathetic. She would never have been separated willingly from her coat in these conditions. No one bothered to reply; they did not know what to say.

'We must look carefully round the banks' said Vadoma. 'Please everyone, we must find her!' But the howling wind was hurling our words to the sky and it was barely possible to hear the person next to you, let alone those further down the line. Vadoma, Alison and I started to search the debris around the bank, while those at the far end of the line drifted further away into the woods, not having heard the news of our find.

The trees still showed no mercy, petulantly thrashing in the gale as the rain beat down onto the paths which looked as if they were boiling like a pan over a fire; and the water was rushing down the hill, creating a shambles of mini-rivers. Our clothes, inadequate for such wild country weather, were starting to snag and shred as brambles and lower branches got caught in sleeves and hoods, tearing them open and letting in more cold and rain.

Not far down the bank we came to an ancient oak tree which had been uprooted in the turmoil. It had toppled to earth like the corpse of some great slaughtered beast, and now lay on its side with half its mighty root structure pointing to the sky. But Vadoma was not looking at the oak tree. She was gazing at the crushed wreckage beneath it, eyes staring.

Rufus and Muffin, sniffing behind us, ran up to the tree. Rufus suddenly stopped, stiff-legged, head and eyes quivering. Then he leaped forward and started scrabbling and barking at a bush which lay partially squashed under the colossal weight of the trunk.

Vadoma followed the dogs down the slope into the hollow. She had seen something. I heard a soft moan escape her lips: 'Not Marianna, please not, please not!'

'Alison! Reg!' I shouted. 'The dogs have found something!'

They both rushed over and together we approached the bushes. Partially concealed below the shattered branches was a pale shape; I could make out the colour of pale human skin. I lifted one of the branches away and saw Marianna's golden hair, now soaked and filthy, trailing downward.

'I wouldn't look too close' said Reggie. 'Looks like something's attacked her.'

I pulled gingerly at one of Marianna's trailing arms, hoping beyond all rational hope that somehow she would come to life at my touch, cough and splutter and tell us all she was OK. As I pulled, the remains of Marianna's slim form came free of the branches and rolled over towards us, facing us.

Vadoma let out a scream. Alison sobbed and put her hand to her mouth.

We were looking at the staring face of a corpse. Around Marianna's stomach was a terrible, gaping, bloodied cavity. She had been disembowelled. And her once-lovely mouth was now frozen open in a grimace of pain and terror. Even worse, those wonderful blue, blue eyes were gone. All that was left were two gaping, bloody, empty sockets.

My mind was a blur of wild thoughts, shocked images. Marianna's body, once so beautiful, lay before me naked for the first time, the remnants of its beauty streaming in blood and weed, disgustingly, shockingly mutilated. Who, or what, could have done this?

Vadoma sank to the ground, shaking and sobbing

uncontrollably, Alison clutching her and moaning softly in shock.

Piers and Wendy now came running up. Don't look' said Alison firmly, but she was a second too late. They recoiled with a roar of shock and disgust.

Reggie was already on his radio phone, calling for help. 'Yes, ambulance, quick as you like' I heard him say. 'Confirmed fatality, female.'

There was nothing more we could do for poor Marianna. I cursed myself for having let her out of our sight. In shock we trudged back in ones and twos, barely giving a thought to our physical condition.

The village had claimed its first death.

CHAPTER TWENTY ONE

That evening was a sombre affair. The Howarths had limped back home to recover in the city, but we now had three new guests, having invited Fonso, Esmeralda and Florika to move in with us. Their caravan would not be usable again for some time, and more seriously they feared their community faced being broken up and scattered to the four corners of the land following the virtual destruction of the site. Fonso feared it was unlikely that they would ever gather together again as they had.

Alison and I, having done the best we could to console Vadoma and the children about the loss of Marianna, went to work repairing the damage that had been done by the storm and the darker forces we had encountered. We had spent much time with the police, making statements and trying to give them some clues which might eventually enable them to trace Marianna's family. It would take many weeks to track down her roots; we knew next to nothing about her background or even which town she originally came from.

Only Granny, in her own strange world as always, seemed relatively cheerful. She was now working flat out to replenish her supply of charms and protective plants around the house.

'Now, we must have more rowan, angelica and bay' she instructed us. 'Vadoma is getting some fresh birch and yew twigs. You have to carry them with you all the time.'

'It's hardly practical, Mum' said Alison wearily 'They haven't done us much good so far, have they?'

'The spirits will come!' countered Granny with a wagging finger. 'They will seek vengeance!' She rolled her eyes melodramatically. She had a faraway look, as if travelling back over the centuries to capture the wisdom of lost generations who had seen all this before. Vadoma did not challenge her. She grasped her hand in sympathy to show her support. Fonso and Esmeralda did not smile; they shared the belief. I did not shake my head contemptuously as I might once have done. I had learned to respect these mysterious forces.

Granny was proved right all too soon. Deep in the watches of that night I awoke, knowing that something more than the haunting quaver of a distant owl or the bark of a dog had disturbed me. That feeling of coldness was back, and now I could hear muffled footsteps and distant voices. Shadows seemed to be moving outside the window and something flicked past the bedroom door.

Then I heard a sob; the sound of a soul in torment, grieving or mourning.

I slipped quietly out of bed, trying not to wake Alison, steeling myself for yet another encounter with forces beyond our understanding. I wrapped my dressing gown tightly around me, but it gave no answer to the psychological chill which had enveloped me.

Out in the corridor I almost collided with Fonso, who had clearly also heard something.

'Seems quiet enough now' he said. But we could both feel the cold silence, the brooding stillness which pervaded the house.

'This house is the centre of a whole range of psychic activity' he said. 'Esmeralda felt it as soon as we arrived. Some houses have walls which seem to absorb spirit-energy and then release it later - it's like a recording. I suspect bad things have happened here. Do you know much about its history?'

'We know a witchfinder lived here about four hundred years ago. Steve seems to know all about it. He was telling us this man used to force confessions through the most horrible tortures. Apparently he used the bodies for all kinds of sickening medical purposes. He wouldn't tell me the detail, or rather I wouldn't let him, but it seems it was something to do with finding the secret of perpetual life. It all seems a bit far-fetched, although after what's happened I'm not so sure.'

'Hush a minute!' interjected Fonso. 'Listen.'

We could both hear a strange whispering sound, like disembodied voices around us in the dark. It did not feel hostile or threatening; it seemed to be a continuous weave of sound within which no words were distinguishable, like the gentle lapping of waves on a shingle beach. As it grew louder we became aware of footsteps softly approaching us.

'Don't move' whispered Fonso. The steps seemed to be passing down the corridor towards the room which had been Marianna's.

And then we saw them, mere fluctuations in the light at first, then pale, shifting shadows in the gloom. There seemed to be an endless procession of them, all making their way in a silent line. Some were coming down the stairs from the attic, while others seemed to be joining them from the stairs down to the hall. There were more which must have come through the kitchen from the cellar.

But we could tell that these were gentle, benign spirits. The dogs had either failed to notice them or had been pacified by their peaceful aura. It was as if the spirits of horrors past had come to offer solace to Marianna. They carried an atmosphere of sadness and melancholy, as if their souls were being held back from the sanctuary of a gentle death.

As the forms grew clearer I could see that some of them were broken or damaged; some were missing limbs or eyes and many had gaping holes in their stomachs. Others appeared to have been flayed. It was shocking and repellent, yet I felt sorrow for them in their plight.

Just then Vadoma joined us on the landing. I looked at her in alarm and put out an arm to protect her and hold her back, but she did not seem shocked or frightened. On her face was a look of deep sadness and understanding.

By now all the adults were awake and joining us to stand frozen in the corridor as we all witnessed this fantastic passage of souls. The figures were so diaphanous, so translucent that they could well have been an invasion of morning mist from the estuary, twisting and turning, slipping effortlessly through ill-fitting doors and windows. What I could not have expected was a new and surprising warmth which seemed to be spreading throughout the house, pushing out the terrible winter chill which had cursed us.

But then, as if a switch had been flicked, the cold returned. There was suddenly a crescendo of activity and noise. Trixie, Florika and Ben, who were now sharing a room for mutual comfort, woke up screaming simultaneously, as if from the same nightmare. All the spirits instantly vanished; the house froze in a paralysis of expectation and fear.

Fonso was the first to move. 'Come on, check the children!' he shouted, and we all jerked into action. But even as he spoke, his words were overwhelmed by the return of the storm. Unheralded, it announced its presence with a shattering cacophony of noise and light, as if some earthly event had triggered off a vengeance of blackness and dread to cover the earth.

As we entered the children's room, we saw it again. A massive charge of lightning lit up the sky and there, silhouetted against the window, shimmering in front of the flimsy curtains, was the same spectre in the same wide-brimmed hat I had seen before. I glimpsed him only for a split second before he disappeared.

'It just went straight through us' whispered Vadoma in shock. She pointed to the door and looked pleadingly at Esmeralda for support.

Then from above came a shriek – Granny. I looked up to see her standing like a Valkyrie at the top of the stairs from the attic, brandishing a rowan branch and pointing downwards with a dramatic gesture.

'The kitchen!' she yelled. As she spoke the dogs gave voice to a frantic bedlam of barking.

Vadoma, Fonso and I started down the stairs while Granny began what sounded like a medieval chant of protection, waving her protective plants defiantly at the sky and glaring horribly, as if challenging the spirit to return. 'I know you! I know you!' she was muttering. What she meant by that wasn't clear.

The spirits were swirling around behind Granny in an increasing tumult of movement, indistinguishable, ever changing, yet possessed of a presence and a purpose. They were surging in and out of the attic but seemed to be afraid, or unable, to move past Granny, who appeared to be blocking their way down the stairs which led to the kitchen.

And then it happened. Suddenly behind her there formed a thickening of the greyness, a solid mass coalesced out of the shadows, and Granny seemed to stumble forward. She rolled and pitched headlong down the stairs before any of us could move a muscle to save her. With a sigh she came to rest on the landing with her legs and arms awry, her head resting at an obscene angle on the lowest stair.

Vadoma was instantly there, holding her and pleading with her to wake up. But to no avail.

'She has gone!' Vadoma gasped in shock, and then grief overtook her.

I looked down at Granny's form, so small and shrunken as it seemed now. In death her face bore an expression of calm acceptance, as if in her last seconds she had witnessed something beyond the sight of ordinary mortals.

'I'm sorry love' I said to Alison. She rushed forward and checked her pulse and then her pupils.

'Oh Mum! I can't believe it!' she sobbed.

Just then I noticed something very odd; the house and the storm had fallen instantly and completely silent.

Vadoma, still cradling Granny's white shock of hair, looked up. 'I see her' she said. 'She is torn between her earthly friends and the holy world she now sees. Is not like last time. She is standing in front of an altar. It is very old, all is very old. She has white robe, golden trim.'

'Is she... what, Heaven?'

'Wait! I hear something... voices are singing now. Hymns they are singing. I see many saints! All is white, so much white. But this is good. Is happy!' She turned to Alison, standing in shock and disbelief with her hand over her mouth.

'Your mother, she has found peace, so much peace. She is in cathedral, such a big, big cathedral. I can see more churches outside – you know... spires? This sky is so blue! This is good place. Do not worry. Granny is safe now. She very safe, not worried any more.'

She fell quiet, still deep in that other world, as if she was in direct contact with Granny. We waited, overawed, not wanting to interrupt or break the link she seemed to have formed with another place, another world.

'She is holding a big cup' Vadoma went on. 'It is the sacred chalice. Bread and wine is here. All sharing. Church bells, such lovely bells! Now I see God's family. She is talking to them. Now she is talking to us. She has message! She is saying...

CHAPTER TWENTY ONE

'What is she saying?' sobbed Alison.

'She is saying goodbye. But there is something else... she will see us again. She will see us all again soon.'

CHAPTER TWENTY TWO

Alison and I carried Granny carefully into her room and placed her limp form peacefully on her bed before calling the doctor. Then we plodded downstairs. Esmeralda made some tea and we sat cupping the hot beverage in our hands, barely talking.

Two people had now died in strange circumstances, one horribly, and one tragically young. None of it seemed real.

'You know we have to leave this house, don't you' said Alison in a flat monotone.

'I'm sorry' I said, gripping her hand.

'It's not your fault, Bill. No one could have imagined things like this could happen. This is England, for goodness' sake. It's the bloody 21st century!'

'We'll have to sort a few things out before we go' I said. 'We'll have to sell the damn place. How easy is that going to be?'

'Completely impossible' she replied with mock cheerfulness. 'Do people buy haunted houses these days? We'll soon find out. If not, well, we'll manage, I'm sure. Just have to get some earplugs.'

'You can live with us again when we have a new site' said Esmeralda helpfully.

'Thank you. We may have to take you up on that' said Alison.

'Look, I'm sure Granny just went from old age' I put in.

Alison snorted. 'You saw it. You were there!'

'What are we going to tell the police?'

'How about, 'Granny's gone to heaven'?'

'Do you believe that?'

'Actually, yes'

'So do I. Well, kind of. Don't worry, we'll get through it.'

'Well, there is one thing we can do' volunteered Fonso, looking at Esmeralda. 'All the problems in the house seem to be coming from the cellar, and the shapes we saw outside were going towards the church.'

'Yes. And rumour has it that there is a passage between them. You remember Steve was telling us about that?'.

'Funny you should mention him' said Vadoma. 'Steve has been different since Marianna died. He doesn't seem to want to talk about it. I reckon he really liked her, but she didn't feel the same way.'

'I think we should take a good look at that cellar' said Fonso, steering the conversation back to the practical.

Alison gave me a look, as if to say 'You're on your own on that one'.

'OK' I said, though I couldn't help feeling a lurch of fear deep in my stomach at the thought of what had happened in the cellar last time. 'That back wall.'

'Exactly' said Fonso. 'Got some torches?'

'Should have enough for one each' I replied. 'I did have a look, it seemed completely solid.'

'Let's ask Steve if he'd like to help' ventured Esmeralda. 'He's supposed to be the history expert.' Something in her tone told me she did not entirely trust our charming amateur historian.

'I will go now and ask him, if you really want this' volunteered Vadoma. Her tone suggested that she did not expect Steve to be available.

'OK. In the meantime let's dig out the gardening tools. We'll need picks and shovels, crowbars. Maybe a sledgehammer.'

As expected, Vadoma came back alone. 'They say Steve is off work' she said. 'He won't be at the pub today.'

We gathered a motley bundle of tools old and new and carried them down the steep steps into the cellar. I rigged up some lighting and made sure all the torches had fresh batteries – we didn't want to depend on a few weak low-energy light bulbs. Ben insisted on joining us, despite being told he was far too young.

Esmeralda picked her way down the stairs to join us in the passage.

'This place has history' she murmured, shivering involuntarily.

'It's always cold down here' I told her, but she looked at me as if I had pointed out that it sometimes gets dark at night. She sensed things which were invisible to me and Alison, but she seemed to share her vision with Fonso and Vadoma, both of whom looked pensive in expectation of what we might find.

Finally we had carried all our gear to the back wall of the cellar. Fonso began looking at the brickwork, searching for any signs of irregularity, tapping the wall with a hammer.

'There might be a space behind it somewhere' he said quietly. Then there came a shout from Ben, who had penetrated deeper into the musty depths behind the stairwell.

'I've found some bottles!' he called. 'Granny must have left them there, bet that's where all the gin went.'

'Ben! Don't talk like that about Granny. Show some respect!' I snapped, betraying the tension I was feeling.

'Here we go' said Fonso. 'Listen, can you hear the difference?'

He was tapping a section of brickwork in the far right-hand corner. 'This seems to be more recent' he said. I went over and examined the area he was indicating. The brickwork and the mortar did indeed look relatively fresh.

Now that we had something to attack, we all set to with picks and sledgehammers in an orgy of destruction. The looseness of the mortar and the brittleness of the bricks became apparent very quickly. After a few hefty smacks from the sledgehammer a cobweb of cracks opened up and we could hear broken masonry falling away on the far side.

'There must be a gap' I said. 'Another room.'

'There must have been a door here' Esmeralda pointed out. 'When you hear of spirits going through solid walls, invariably there was once a door or a gate there which they were using when they were alive.'

Then Fonso gave a mighty swing with the sledgehammer and a large block of brickwork fell inwards, leaving a black and gaping hole. From it floated the smell of centuries of bottled-up staleness, an odour of dust and earth mingled with noisome traces of putrescence, death and decay. We must surely now be close to the cold, corrupt heart of the evil which had been invading the Manor over the past months.

I picked up the big torch, took a deep breath of the fresher air away from the hole, and stepped forward. Through the gap I could make out a passageway stretching into the distance. As I shone the beam around, swarms of rats scurried away into the shadows and pairs of tiny, silvery, predatory eyes were reflected back from the recesses. Watching. And waiting.

'Let's open it up properly' said Fonso. 'We're going to need to go inside. Looks like this is where all that activity happened.' I could not help feeling apprehensive of the horrors which might lurk there.

We set to, pulling and pushing the ancient brickwork until there was a hole large enough to squeeze through. Suddenly Rufus and Muffin exploded into activity, breaking away to leap through the hole to disappear into the dark beyond. Their barking and scuffing echoed back down the passageway towards us with an unearthly mixture of growls and grunts; more fearful because the sounds exploded out of the darkness where we knew the rodents and perhaps even the spirits we'd seen were biding their time.

We started down the tunnel. The walls were of ancient

bricks and a vaulted ceiling, also of brickwork, arched over us from the walls on either side. Everywhere we smelled decay. In places great chunks of masonry had fallen down to cover parts of the floor.

Then abruptly from out of the dark flew two shapes; the dogs. They fled past us, ears flat and tails between their legs, jumped through the hole in the wall and were up the cellar steps in a split second.

'Ben, go with the dogs to see they're all right' I said.

'He can't go on his own' said Esmeralda. 'Come on Ben, let's go and tell Mum what we've found.' I listened to their footsteps echoing back towards the stairway. Suddenly the place seemed more desolate and sinister than ever.

Fonso and I pushed on down the passageway, carefully climbing over the piles of debris, talking quietly so as not to disturb the place any further. I could not help thinking that too much disturbance might cause the whole structure to collapse.

'Any idea which way we're going?' said Fonso.

'The cellar stairway faces – let's see – south, so we must be heading towards the church' I replied. 'We're going to hit the cemetery if this goes on.' I felt my heart palpitating in a continuation of the fear of the unknown lurking in the dark as we invaded their resting place. The anticipation of meeting animal or spirit forms which thrived in this place, feeding off the putrid flesh of those who had passed away, filled me with horror.

Just then Fonso's torch revealed a gaping hollow to the left of the passageway. I joined him and we peered into it. It seemed to be some sort of alcove, stretching away for several yards into the blackness. I swung the torch around to reveal another alcove, almost opposite. Further on were more of them, leading off the main tunnel at regular intervals.

Fonso examined the first one with his torch. It was perhaps two feet high and the same wide. It had been carefully cut and extended many yards back into the earth.

'What on earth are these for?' muttered Fonso.

Many of the holes had been blocked by falling debris, but the fifth we came to appeared to be intact. By leaning in and shining the torch at the roof, I could see that every few yards there were dark holes in the roof and above them could be glimpsed fragments of what appeared to be filthy wooden boarding, now broken, rotten and distorted. The smell of decay was stronger than ever.

Fonso rocked back on his heels, his breath escaping with a hiss.

'My God, they're coffins' he said. 'They've been robbing the graves from beneath.'

I remembered the stories of Joshua's experiments on human bodies to find the secret of everlasting life. He had needed a supply of specimens to study. Now we knew how he had obtained some of them.

I was speechless from shock.

No wonder there was such an atmosphere of violation and malevolence in this benighted place. I imagined souls wandering in perpetuity, denied a peaceful burial, the biblical wailing and gnashing of teeth. And these were the 'respectable' dead. I shuddered to think of the vengeance and retribution due to the witchfinder from all those who had been less lucky in life, and who, being cursed in death, had ended up on the north side of the church, in unconsecrated ground.

As we looked further down the passage, we could see that a part of it branched off, the floor here beginning to slope downwards as if into the bowels of the earth. It was completely blocked by a roof collapse, so we could explore it no further.

'This part must head down towards the estuary' said Fonso. 'Perhaps it was a smugglers' route to hide the contraband after they'd brought it ashore. That means there ought to be a storage area somewhere.'

'We can't check that out now' I said. 'We'll never move all that mud and rubble.'

I was starting to feel that it was all too much for me, but Fonso seemed to be in his element. There was an enthusiasm in his voice which I could not share. I would gladly have left this exploration to others.

Then I heard a rustle in the corner and nearly jumped out of my skin. I felt myself beginning to shake slightly. Now, I knew, I had had enough. An attack by a pack of rats, or worse, would be one excitement too many. I realised that I had, yet again, begun to tremble. Suddenly I found I could not get the idea of the rats out of my head. I had always had a distaste for the creatures bordering on phobia, and while I could handle an encounter with one or two, the idea of massed ranks of them made my knees turn to jelly and my throat turn dry from fear. I saw them lying in ambush, waiting patiently in anticipation until the batteries in the torches failed, and then swarming quietly in their hundreds in the darkness over our helpless, screaming bodies, mobbing us in a frenzy of vindictive fearlessness, inflicting death by endless bites, clinging with their teeth to our writhing bodies until we were still. I felt in my mind the pain of claws and teeth as the brown, disease-ridden bodies suffocated us in the darkness, sharp noses penetrating our soft inner organs to seek out the tastiest morsels while we beat our arms vainly in a hopeless attempt to cling to life, like a helpless calf being overwhelmed and slowly eaten alive by a pack of wolves. Then our corpses, frozen in the rictus of agonising death, would lie there in the dust of ages, to be rendered within days to skeletons like those in the catacombs, the bones dismembered, fought over, strewn like building rubble along these godforsaken passageways of hell. I was subsumed by a mindless panic which would have been uncontrollable in the dark and was barely manageable even with Fonso's reassuring presence and the light from our torches.

'Come on, just a bit further' said Fonso. He pointed his torch further into the gloom and we saw yet more narrow, lateral tunnels.

'Here, what's this?' said Fonso. 'This is a bigger one.'

He was peering into a larger recess which concealed a low, arched entrance. Beyond the arch was a great oaken door, studded with iron knobs. He gave it a tentative push, but it appeared immovable.

'Must be something that matters behind that' I said trying to master the tremble in my voice.

'We'll come back to it later' he said. 'I bet it's the smugglers' storage chamber.'

We moved on through the dark until we were well within the pagan burial chambers. Now we began to see not just the remnants of coffins but of the bodies they had contained. I was deeply glad Alison and the children were not with us. There were loose arm bones, ribs and thighs and some partial skeletons, all white and long since stripped of their decayed flesh. There were no signs of mummified flesh or hair, a testament to the depredations of rats and other vermin over the centuries. Where the roof debris had piled up, white shards were everywhere, many scarred by the grooves of small, sharp teeth.

Presently we came across another wall, but this one was different. From the mixture of mud and brickwork it had to be of even greater antiquity. And it completely blocked the passageway.

'Well, I think that's a pretty successful afternoon' I said to Fonso. My unspoken message was that I'd had enough. I wanted desperately to get out of this hellhole and back into the world of living, breathing human beings, to Alison and the children.

'Maybe, let's see' said Fonso, and leaned heavily against the middle section. The wall immediately caved in, crumbling with a crash of collapsing masonry and clouds of dust. We both coughed desperately to drive the foul dust from our noses and lungs. At last we had recovered enough to see what the settling dust had revealed; yet another tunnel.

'Come on' said Fonso, stepping through the debris left by the remains of the wall. I followed unwillingly, but it was instantly clear that this tunnel was different. It seemed to be much cleaner, with far less of an impression of mess and decay. Even the air smelled better. The stench of death and corruption was less obvious. It was as if this area was from a more gentle time, when the dead had been treated more respectfully.

We advanced slowly, exploring with our torches. Here the bones had been stacked in a much more orderly manner, with some corpses still lying in individual coffins. In one room, stacks of bones had been systematically assembled in methodical mounds.

'You know where we are?' said Fonso. 'It's the catacombs. The church must be just above us. There should be a spiral staircase at the far end of the corridor which leads up to the altar.'

'So we've found it - the tunnel between the church and the Manor. It's a pity Steve isn't here, he'd be really interested in this.' Now that I knew what we had achieved I was beginning to feel better about the whole adventure.

'We need to open that door' said Fonso.

'All in good time' I said. 'Right now I would kill for a cup of tea.'

'Something a bit stronger than tea' said Fonso.

'Damn right.'

CHAPTER
TWENTY THREE

'If you're going to have to force an old door open, shouldn't you get help from a builder?' said Alison. 'At least you ought to tell Reg. You don't know what you're going to find.'

Both Fonso and Esmeralda, their kind having centuries of conflict with the establishment behind them, thought this was a bad idea.

'We should keep this to ourselves for now' said Fonso. 'I don't think we ought to spread it around, not yet.'

'There could be real treasures' I suggested. 'Gold and jewels, priceless relics. We could be...'

'Bill, pull yourself together' snapped Alison. She knew my mind was already starting to wander over a whole range of impossible and ridiculous scenarios.

So, leaving the dogs in the kitchen and the children safely upstairs, the five of us hauled some additional tools, plus a box of candles, down the stairs and into the cellar. That dreadful, airless stench had now begun to dissipate, leaving a much healthier atmosphere than the miasma we had encountered when we had opened up the passage. Yet there still lurked an intangible sense of slumbering horror, a dormant melancholy lingering in that darkness of perpetual night. I imagined an invisible army of souls split between life and death, resigned to an underworld of gloom and despair, ever waiting and hoping for someone, something, to release their spirits and let them fly free.

'The lock is probably old and rusty' said Fonso. 'It ought to break quite easily.' I was happy to defer to his greater experience and passed him the crowbar, which he pushed into the gap between the brickwork and the door, next to the lock. He heaved, and we heard something creak.

'Watch out' he said. He heaved again, this time putting all his weight on the crowbar. As he did so there came a thundering crack and the whole door split in two and fell to the floor in a shower of debris.

'That was easy enough!' he laughed. We kicked the wreckage of the door away and looked in, to see an extraordinary sight.

'My god, we've found the library!' Alison gasped.

I looked around. By the light of our torches, I could see she was right. The room was too big for us to see its extent, but everywhere we directed the torches we saw books; ancient, dust-covered volumes, all looking as if they had been there for centuries.

'Let's light the candles' said Vadoma. She pushed past us into the room. We lit candles and positioned them every few yards on the uneven, compacted earth floor. Now we could see the full extent of the room.

We stepped back to try to make sense of what we saw. It was a very long room running parallel to the main passageway, so it must clearly lie right beneath the kitchen garden and extend towards the church. Two huge tables of solid oak dominated the space in the middle, and upon this were many books. Some were open and disintegrating, others were piled high in great stacks. Among them were maps, charts and drawings.

In the centre of the table was a large sheet of parchment displaying a diagram of the human body, showing muscle structure and internal organs. The edges of it were anchored flat by what appeared to be leg bones.

Down the main wall against the passageway were shelves of ancient books bound in disintegrating leather, with some particularly large ones bound in wood. On top of the books and in empty spaces were many pamphlets and drawings, some of them rolled up and held together by tattered and crumbling ribbons. Most of the bookcases seemed to contain volumes on science and natural history.

The opposite wall was divided into arches, guarding recesses like the alcoves of a wine cellar. Within these were more tables and chairs, which, having been made of softer wood, had largely rotted to nothing.

'Just look at this!' said Vadoma in awe. She had found some illustrations of mythical creatures which had been bound together into a medieval bestiary. Although the binding had deteriorated, the illuminated pictures were still sharp and richly-coloured.

'These are on vellum' Esmeralda pointed out. 'That's made from some sort of leather or hide. I wonder what animal they used? You can feel the thickness and softness of the pages. It seems very fine.' Then she suddenly froze and stopped stroking, recoiling in horror.

'Oh my god, it's human skin' she muttered.

'My God!' said Alison. 'Are you sure?'

'Look, you can see the pattern of a chest.'

I looked more closely. It was true; the wrinkles and folds matched exactly the pattern of a chest.

I turned to another book. 'Look at these sketches of the human body' I said. 'They must have used the bodies from the graveyard to learn all this. And all those executed witches, criminals and smugglers which the witchfinder found guilty.'

I felt Alison shudder beside me. The horror of centuries past seemed to be standing at our shoulders, as if the practices of a long distant era had closed in and caught up with us, intruders who should not be there.

The sketches were in a rotting cloth and board folio about eighteen inches tall and twelve inches wide. There must have been fifty pages of detailed drawings of anatomy in a dull brown ink. There were pages which dealt with the muscle structure around the backbone, pages which drew arms and legs flexing in different positions, pages which focused on the skeletal structure and more gruesome ones which showed cross sections of organs. Eyes, liver and heart could be identified. All were accompanied by lines of scribbled text which were too faded to read in the light of the candles.

The drawings had clearly been made from life; or rather, from death. The detail was superb. Although the paper was badly perished in parts with large areas of brown foxing, there was still enough remaining to identify the illustrations.

Visible on the outer front cover were the words:

MORS TUA VITA MEA

'Your death, my life' said Vadoma. 'They believed you keep your life if you take life of another. Maybe this explain what happen here. The alchemists were trying to extend life, but first, they must understand how life work. They kill to get bodies to study. God made humans to die; this his gift to get to heaven. You not die, you not go to heaven, so to find everlasting life was heresy. Very dangerous, but they not mind risk'

Vadoma had put it in a nutshell. She had a thirst for knowledge which allowed her to sponge up everything she'd heard or read about, and by listening to Steve over the last few months she had clearly learned a great deal.

Alison nodded agreement. 'The alchemists believed it was possible to live forever. If we look at the advances in medicine over the last fifty years or so, maybe they were right. We have cloned animals, we understand the genome, we can create new limbs from stem cells. Life has been extended enormously. Maybe one day we will not need to die at all.'

'Medicine can't stop ageing' I offered. 'Immortality is a long way off. And how would we find room for everyone if there was no death?'

Just then came a shout from Fonso, who was exploring the furthest alcove.

'Hey, look at this! There's another room through here.' We walked down the length of the room in the wavering candlelight, but before we reached Fonso my eye was caught by another great tome resting on a table, bound in wood with a heavy brass clasp holding the covers closed. On the front cover was written, only just legible, in faded gold lettering:

ACHERUNTIS PABULUM

'OK Vadoma, you're our Latin scholar. What does this mean?' I asked.

'Not sure' she looked puzzled. 'But Acheron was river in hell and pabulum means food. Perhaps a book about people who were condemned to be executed, now on their way to hell? Bring candle closer please.'

The cover was immensely heavy and as I eased the book open the spine started to crack and pop. There were many pages of vellum, most of which had warped and perished. They bore countless columns filled with ancient brown writing. The text appeared to be by the same hand as that which had written the descriptions in the last book of drawings, with alchemy notes in the margins.

'I can't read this, it's too faded. I need to find a page which has survived better' I said. 'The ink has smeared and the letters have merged.'

Esmeralda said nothing. She was looked at the book with a shocked expression on her face. But the rest of us were too involved to notice.

At last I found a page which was relatively undamaged. It was divided into three columns with a name in the first. The second column contained descriptions of crimes of which they had been accused, while the third detailed the punishment. *'William Attwell… did steal Meat of Fowle… hanged alive'* read one. *'Mary Bridewell… caused Malicious Harm unto a Rival… Confessed under Torture, Tongue cut Out and Hanged'* said another.

As I read on, the horror and the self-indulgence of recording such brutal justice began to unfold. Many of the crimes listed were patently absurd. The local communities had been stripped of children or babies who had been born sick or deformed, or who later became crippled through accidents, or those who were 'simple' in mind. They had been cruelly abducted from their families and then tortured and condemned to death. Their agonies and their wailing and beseeching for mercy had been ignored. The magistrate's interpretation that God's demand for absolution could only be achieved through pain and death overrode all other considerations. Some babies had comments about the 'sins of their fathers' being explanation enough for their deformities or mental derangement, and adequate justification for punishment and death.

The catalogue of torture went on and on, with several lines being devoted to witchcraft causing crop failure and making cattle barren. The punishment, after interrogation and torture, was always hanging.

'Look at this one' pointed out Fonso, looking over my shoulder. His finger was hovering over some lines near the bottom of the page. 'We saw this man during the last great storm.'

Esmeralda nodded, as if seeing long-dead people was only to be expected. I studied the entry. It referred to a miller who had been accused of mixing sawdust with his flour and had been sentenced to be strapped to his waterwheel '*which should revolve slowly until he did dye*'. His family had been evicted to wander the lanes and hedgerows, while his land and buildings had reverted to the local squire - who was also the magistrate and witchfinder.

There was a further entry for this one. The body had been lost and the water bailiff had been instructed to search the riverbank and estuary and to return it to the magistrate for 'suitable disposal.' However it seemed that the body had never been recovered, so his spirit had been left to roam the land searching for resolution, somehow to rejoin his family in the other world.

The list went on and on; tinkers being savaged by starved dogs, children locked into the village stocks for paltry offences, strangers disappearing without trace. We became speechless as the horrors continued to emerge.

I suggested quietly to Fonso 'Let's go and look at the room you've found. It can't be worse than this.'

But I had spoken too soon.

CHAPTER TWENTY FOUR

Fonso had found a flimsy-looking brick and flint archway which looked as if it might collapse at any moment. Rubble was piled on the floor, partially blocking the entrance, and the walls of the arch were bulging inwards as if the weight of the ground above was too much.

Directed by his torch, I stepped through into the new space - and felt a wave of nausea as the putrid smell of death hit me once again. It was a hammer blow after the relative peace of the library. I felt as if all the breath had been sucked out of my body. The candles flared and guttered, burning greenish and then orange as if assailed by strange gases.

'Put the candles on the floor' said Fonso. 'Spread them out so we can see.'

We shone our torches around the room to reveal an extraordinary scene. It was like an old fashioned apothecary's lair, the walls lined by shelves bearing huge quantities of glass jars. The room was dominated by a heavy wooden table, perhaps nine feet long and two feet wide. It was clearly no dining table, nor did it look as if it had been used for studying books or maps, as in the library. It was not flat, for a start. A roughly-curved trough ran down the centre, and the entire surface looked as if it had been jabbed, sliced and gouged by countless knives. It was filthy with dark, brownish stains.

'It's like an old-fashioned butcher's block' Alison observed.

'That's exactly what it is' said Esmeralda. 'But not for animals.' Her voice was shaking.

'There's a hole in the middle' I pointed out. 'I suppose that's...'

'To allow the blood to run away' finished Fonso.

There was an awful silence as the ramifications of our discovery became clear. It seemed hard to believe.

We looked around the room to see that the candlelight was revealing more torments. Three of the walls bore rows of heavy wooden shelves upon which were more glass jars filled with liquid. Within them floated all manner of nameless abominations.

I took a step closer. I knew immediately what they must be, but it still came as a terrible shock to see, within those jars, a hellish assortment of human body parts, or portions of body parts. In one was a human heart, so well preserved that I could almost imagine I saw it still beating. Another contained a pair of kidneys; yet more had lumps of glutinous flesh which had decayed into nameless balls of viscous matter, floating in the preservers' alcohol in a perpetual suspension of ghastliness.

I heard Alison gasp in shock and disgust. I wanted to turn away myself, but I could not resist the urge to see more, to know what it was that these people had felt it necessary to preserve.

One entire shelf was devoted to brains; dozens of them, some so small that they must clearly have been ripped from the skulls of small children. There were shelves of lungs, shelves of livers, severed limbs standing in tall jars, smaller bottles containing hands, fingers and feet.

On the lower shelves or standing on the dusty floor were more glass containers, much bigger ones. These held what must have been the by-products of experimentation, all hovering in murky fluids. We could see the grotesque results of body grafting; a cat's head attached to a dog's body, a bat's wings sewn on to the trunk of a stoat. It was a chaotic mixture of animal and human bodies, combined by some crude art to make monsters which defied imagination. There were bodies with extra limbs, animals with multiple heads. Worst of all, there were entire corpses of deformed children, their eyes bleakly open and mouths screaming against the glass.

In the corners stood dozens of terracotta amphorae, containing we knew not what further horrors. We dared not lift their lids.

The room was suffused with an atmosphere of deathly despair. The walls seemed to radiate a sense of bitter anger; the pent-up desperation of so many poor souls who had been so horribly treated and whose spirits had been unable to claim sanctuary. It was as if the walls themselves were releasing memories of what they had witnessed. We looked on with speechless loathing. But yet, there was a faint hint of hope. The flickering candlelight seemed to carry a whispering warmth in the half-light of misery as the spirits tried to bridge into our world from the distant past; or perhaps it was the will to live which gave premonition that vengeance, and closure, was nearer.

And then we got to the final wall.

Leaning against it were several wooden frames punctured by holes every few inches. They seemed to be there to anchor strings to stretch material over the frame, like the skin of a drum. Next to them were piles of what looked like horse dung, but it was solidified by age and desiccation, although some of it bore a light covering of what looked like fungus or mould; a grisly symbiosis in the cold and dark. Further along was a large stack of what looked like small rotting, leather blankets, which had stiffened and fused into one mass. At the edges we could discern the marks of rats' teeth.

'My god, you know what this is?' said Esmeralda. 'They were making vellum pages for the library. I felt this when I touched that book.' she pointed back to the first room. 'They would have used the dung and probably lime from the estuary to loosen the hair while the skins were being soaked in the bins. And then the frames were used to stretch the skins to dry them, and to scrape off the flesh'.

'But they use human skin!' mumbled Vadoma in a flash of understanding. She had sensed Esmeralda's shock on touching the library books, and now saw deeply into the past. 'Those spirits in the forest, during the storm? They were going to the church, collecting more souls again as they passed down the hill. They have no skin, many of them, no arms sometimes. Someone take their skin, take their arms, take their... organs. They bring those parts here, keep them for ever'.

'And what is worse is that the best vellum comes from stillborn animals, or very young ones' added Esmeralda gently. 'That is why we have found so many young children in these jars.'

We all fell silent, filled with a shared sense of outrage and pity for those unfortunate dead, most of whom were too young to have had any chance to experience joy in life.

And then, hidden behind one of the bins, we came across a frame with a square of what could only have been fresh skin stretched across it. While we were staring at this, our minds frozen, the candles flamed unexpectedly and we saw another jar high on a shelf above the darkness which had been unshadowed for just an instant.

'That one looks quite recent' said Esmeralda. She directed her torch up at the jar and peered at it. It was free of dust. Inside it was a golden liquid, which seemed to have something floating in it.

Vadoma joined her and looked curiously into the jar. Then she reeled back, emitting the most unearthly scream I had ever heard from a human mouth.

I stepped forward, hardly daring to look, but drawn on by sheer curiosity.

There, floating in the liquid, were two enormous eyes, magnified by the thickness of the glass. Human eyes; blue eyes.

I cried out involuntarily. 'Marianna!' We looked at each

other with minds completely numbed; our bodies rigid from shock and the renewal of grief.

'And here is the rest of what they took from her' said Fonso. Beside the jar was a larger one containing something which at first appeared a shapeless mass. With dread, I looked more closely.

'It's her stomach' he said. 'And look at this, beside it.'

Floating in that noxious liquid was an oval shape about the size of a golf ball. I bent to look more closely.

It was a human foetus, perhaps three months old.

Marianna's baby.

'She and Steve must have been closer than we thought' mumbled Alison. 'That evil bastard!'

Vadoma let out a terrible sob.

'Come on, we must get out of here, quickly' I said. 'We need to report all this.'

We trudged wordlessly back the way we had come, none of us looking to right or left, Vadoma weeping helplessly.

CHAPTER TWENTY FIVE

We were a quiet and subdued group that evening. After leaving the cellar, the underground passage and the rooms of horror, we called Reg. He was there within half an hour with two officers from county HQ. They were down there less than five minutes before they came back white faced and tight-lipped.

'We're going to secure the cellar so no one can gain access' said the senior man. 'No one is to try to go down there again under any circumstance.' We were unlikely to challenge that order.

'We'll make sure the far end of the passage complex is equally secure' he went on. 'Your vicar's going to have a bit of a shock. We'll be back with a scene of crime team tomorrow. We need to get the authorities down here to look at the library as well.'

Fonso shrugged helplessly. 'Only one night to survive' he offered hopefully. The weather forecast was for more storms, and these dark and turbulent nights seemed to stimulate supernatural activity.

But in the event, nightfall led to a quiet evening with no shocks from the weather. Certainly there was a cold moon watching the Earth which drove shafts of blue light through the clouds which, although massing and bulging with rain and latent energy, were hastening across the sky, being chased elsewhere by a growling easterly wind which tormented and punished the tree tops in the forest.

We could see them tossing and writhing beyond the grey bulk of the church which, as usual, stood firm in the moonlight. In the far distance, over the hill fort, we could hear the occasional grumble of thunder and see remote flashes of lightning reflecting off the base of the clouds.

'That should wake the pagan spirits from the battlefields' said Fonso with a macabre sense of timing.

'That's enough' said Alison. 'Let's not tempt fate.' She glanced down at the two dogs, our early warning system, but they seemed to have settled down and were sleeping in their usual corner.

'Come on' said Alison. 'Mum's post mortem tomorrow. That will give us something to think about. God forbid they find something they don't like. Now, let's get some sleep.'

I will never know just what it was that woke me that night. There were no unusual sounds, other than the creaking of timber as the beams and rafters expanded and contracted; we had become used to this, for all old houses speak with such voices. There was a gentle patter of rain on the windows, and when I got out of bed to look out of the window I saw there was no frost on the ground, and the garden was bathed in the melancholy blue of the early-hours moonlight. Nothing seemed overtly wrong, yet I knew that unseen forces were once again awakening.

Further afield towards the estuary, I could see that the sea mist was starting to gather. It was forming an immense wall of whirling shadows, dancing, merging and slowly rolling inland, covering everything in an impenetrable blanket. It looked almost solid, yet the outer fringes had teeming fingers which moved in unison as if they were propelling the mass along an unseen path. To join a similar body which was rising from the woods; to mingle and consolidate.

I shivered and turned to go back to the warm sanctuary of Alison and our bed, but before I could do so the dogs started barking. This was not the friendly voice of welcome but an uncontrolled panic of snarling and howling; a warning of invasion. Something was very wrong.

As I went into the corridor I almost bumped into Vadoma coming out of her room. 'What is happening down there?' I asked as we moved quickly down the stairs and crossed the hall to the kitchen.

'I don't know. It is so cold' she said, drawing her dressing gown tightly around her.

I opened the kitchen door to see Rufus and Muffin standing rigidly in their corner with their backs to the wall, as if they couldn't get far enough away. Their tails were between their legs and the hair on their backs was standing stiffly upright. Their attention seemed to be directed at the window overlooking the garden.

'What is it? What do you see?' I asked, almost expecting an

answer. More practically, Vadoma had grabbed the carving knife from the knife block and was grasping it in her slender hand. We looked through the window to see that a grey cloak of fog had quietly and insidiously enveloped the house. It seemed to be finding the cracks and gaps in the old window frame, for wisps of mist were now seeping into the kitchen. Instead of evaporating, they seemed to be growing more real, more solid by the second. Soon we found ourselves staring into a dense cloud of something evanescent, yet almost solid, almost alive. Vadoma gasped and I stood rooted to the spot.

And then we saw a figure. A tall man with piercing eyes emerged from the mist and stood facing us. He was clad in a heavy brown cloak which covered what looked like 17th century breeches and high, soft knee boots. He wore a large-brimmed hat which covered his face.

'My work must go on!' he hissed. Then he took a step towards Vadoma... a step? It was more like a wafting of the mist. As he moved he drew a straight sword which had been hanging within its scabbard on his left hip. He looked up and stared straight into my eyes, and then at last I recognised him.

'My God, Steve! What...?' I gasped.

'No' said Vadoma icily at my side. 'This is not Steve. It is Joshua, the one who used to live here. He has taken Steve's form to deceive us. I saw this man in the courthouse with Granny. I was with her. That's why she shouted 'I know you!' before she died – she saw him and recognised him. That is why she was pushed.'

I could not make sense of what she was telling me, and now

my stomach was tight from fear and paralysis, my mind unable to function. But then Vadoma moved forward quickly with the carving knife raised, and the dogs seemed to recover and hurl themselves at our ghostly visitor. But by the time they had reached him. He had vanished.

'I don't understand' I wailed.

'Steve can move between worlds and has many identities, but that was Joshua. He has come home. I have heard about these people who can travel between worlds.'

As my mind was struggling with such an impossible concept, we heard a scream - Alison.

'He's in the children's room!' she shrieked. The terror in her voice jarred me back to the present. We both raced through the hall, but now we found that somehow the mist had invaded the rest of the house. The hall was bathed in a grey, swirling fog. As we desperately tried to find our way through it to the stairs, it became thicker, and form and structure began to emerge from the shifting shadows. There were distorted shapes curling into images, which began to get steadily clearer. They were coming down from the attic, along the passageway from Marianna's room, up the stairs from the hallway in a never-ending stream. Together they moved soundlessly out of the kitchen and across the hall.

Towards the children's room.

'They are coming to help' murmured Vadoma. 'They are responding to the cry of a mother. It is a desperate prayer which can summon help from sources which we no longer understand'.

I fell back in shock. On the landing, Fonso and Esmeralda could only look on as the misty shapes flowed around them and through them on their way to the children's room. And downstairs the same was happening. Vadoma and I were just spectators to this horror. All around were shadows drifting and floating in the mist. They seemed to disintegrate and reform as the mist moved in a random fashion; a blurred profusion of activity. But yet they appeared to be strengthening as suddenly we could see faces and torsos. The faces were partly formed with features which were indistinct; gaping holes for mouths; small black caverns for eyes with flesh which hung loosely on the ephemeral shapes. Where there was no flesh a yawning rictus left a grimace of internal organs and muscles which pumped and pulsed to their own rhythm. And where there were no internal organs a dark cave of slimy emptiness was a reminder of tortures past. But still they moved onwards in silence, to give succour to those for whom they had been called.

And then there came a long drawn-out shriek which echoed from the tormented depths of hell itself. It carried such intensity of despair and anger that even the mist seemed to freeze for a moment. Then, bursting out from the children's room, came the dark form of Joshua, his sword flailing, cutting and carving through the phantoms in an orgy of attempted destruction. But the wraiths were unaffected while the mist retreated and reformed. They simply swirled and drifted around him as he flailed in terror and desperation in a futile attempt to find substance. Where heads and arms were severed, they simply dispersed, recovered and re-attached themselves back from whence they came. And while this was happening, Joshua was moving down the stairs, across the hall and back to his subterranean sanctuary in the library and his laboratory.

But now the voices started. A soft whisper of rage; a murmur of retribution. A chance for revenge which had been triggered by Alison's frantic appeal for help. Shapeless, incoherent at first, they began to take form, to join together in harmony until every one of those lost souls was chanting the same word, over and over: *Joshua!* The spirits began to flock en masse down into the cellar, leaving the passageway and hall strangely quiet.

'It's OK' called Alison from upstairs in a trembling voice. 'It's all right. They're still asleep, they're all fine.'

Now Fonso and I felt ourselves borne up in this swirling throng, carried bodily with them down into the cellar. 'We have to go along with this' Fonso gasped. 'Don't fight them!' Even if I had disbelieved him, I would have been powerless to resist.

On we were carried, down the stairs and past those evil relics in the library and on into the laboratory of death. At last we stood in that hellish place, to see, facing us in the centre of the room, the form of Joshua. Surrounded by the throng of vengeful spirits, he was brandishing his sword towards us in a gesture of defiance.

The noise of muttering was becoming ever louder as more and more spirits crowded into the library and spilled over into the passageway. There was an agitation, a moaning of anger in the silvery light which came from we knew not where, but it gave an additional spine-chilling tenor to that ghastly room. Once again we looked upon the deformities, the amputations and the empty vessels which had once been human.

The voices and whisperings became more strident - and then, suddenly, silence. Joshua looked up towards the centre of the crowd. From behind us, a new figure was approaching.

'I wished only to save thee; our family' wailed Joshua at the newcomer. 'To share with thee the gift of everlasting life!'

The spirits parted, and there before us stood - a woman. A tall slender woman with rounded hips and long blonde hair.

'Marianna!' I gasped.

As the crowd of spirits moved aside, I saw again the dreadful sight which had assailed me by the marshes; the gaping cavity of her disembowelled stomach. Decayed flesh hung in strips from barely-concealed bones and tendons. Then she turned her sightless, hollow eyes to me, and I looked away in horror. How could this thing, this relic, this travesty be Marianna?

In her withered, skeletal hand I now saw that she was carrying something; a spray of leaves.

'The rowan!' hissed Fonso at my side. 'She means to anchor his spirit, to destroy it for ever.' I looked on in complete amazement. I wished I had listened to Granny more often; she knew about these things.

As Marianna stepped up to Joshua he started to cringe and

back up against the wall. He made a futile swipe with his sword, but it seemed to have no substance. 'I tried to save you!' he kept repeating.

'You murdered us' said Marianna in a low voice, with no trace now of her accent. 'You used and mutilated me and our child, as you used and mutilated so many others, so many innocent souls. You shall do no more evil!'

Then she steadily lifted the rowan branch, held it level, took a step forward and in one firm movement, drove it into Joshua's body. He yielded soundlessly to the blow, like something half real, half spirit, then slumped, with a faint gasp, into the shadows at the foot of the wall. As we looked on, the pool of darkness which surrounded him seemed to shrink and to melt into the stones. As it did so there came a bright hum of energy, and then a brilliant flash suffused the room. I fell back, dazzled, unable to see. At my side, Fonso let out an involuntary cry. The anchorage of the spirit had taken place.

I stood, clinging to the wall for support, for a moment. Gradually the brilliant light faded and I recovered myself. I looked up to see again the tall form of Marianna. Now she turned slowly from the shadows where Joshua had been and looked at us.

With those beautiful blue eyes.

She was whole again. Not just the eyes but those impossibly white teeth, the blonde hair, the peach-pink complexion, the proud breasts – all were back as before, as if the ghastly events of the last few weeks had been nothing more than a terrible nightmare.

And that was not all. It was as if a whirlwind had passed through that room of death. Jars and bottles lay smashed across the floor, bleeding foul-smelling fluids. One after another, those other-worldly spirits clutched their forms in wonder and relief as they made themselves whole again. Limbs grew back once more, and bones came together. Rents and wounds were mended, skin bloomed intact where it had been torn from the frame beneath it; flesh came up upon them, and skin covered them. And then, in this windless vault, the air moved and the breath came into them and they lived, and stood up upon their feet. Now, at last, those tortured souls could move on, avenged and made whole once again.

Gradually the chamber emptied, the voices fading and growing fainter, melting back into the walls to the places from which their mutilated bodies had been ransacked from their tombs, or drifting on the freshening currents of air back towards their places of rest in the churchyard.

Because their bodies had been made whole again.

Marianna was the last to go. She turned to gaze gently at us with a rapturous smile on her once-again lovely face.

Then we heard an old woman's voice: 'Come, my dear, it's much better here'. That voice was unmistakeable, and it was one I never imagined I would hear again; Granny. She turned to smile fondly at us, and then the two of them faded away and the silvery light dulled and went out.

We were left at last in darkness. But now it was a benign, comforting darkness, a place where peace and justice could reign once again.

CHAPTER TWENTY FIVE

Of Joshua there was no trace; not even a shadow of that dismal life which had brought such misery to his world.

EPILOGUE

The next day dawned quietly, with a warmth and peace we had not felt since our arrival in the village. It was wonderful to stroll around in the early hours with the dogs in the knowledge that they would find nothing more sinister to bark at than the scents of last night's foxes. We even strolled across the north side of the church without either of them turning a hair. Rufus recognised the place and scented his way up to the area of unconsecrated ground with careful circumspection, then turned with wagging tail to look at me as if to say 'It's OK boss, all clear.'

Later, as we went over the events of the previous evening, the doorbell rang. It was Reg, with disturbing news.

'Steve has been found dead in his cottage' he said. 'It looks as if he died from a stab wound to the stomach, though there's no sign of a weapon. It's all a mystery, nothing's been stolen, nothing even disturbed.'

'My god! Where did they find him?'

'He was lying on the floor of his den, the place where he used to study his history books. CID say there are books all over the place about alchemy and occult things. They're wondering if someone broke in, but there's no sign of how they could have done it.'

'Steve had secrets we didn't know about' said Alison. 'I don't suppose they'll ever get to the bottom of it. I'm not sure I want them to.' Just then the phone rang from the study. 'Better get that. Thanks Reg, nice of you to let us know' she said, departing to answer it.

'Will you be staying at the Manor?' Reg asked circumspectly.

'I don't think we've put ourselves through all this just to sell up and go and live on the new estate' I answered. 'Though we're going to have to let the dust settle before we can decide for sure.'

'I'll be taking my leave then, thanking you Mr Cavendish.' He saw himself out.

No sooner had Reg departed than Alison came into the kitchen looking white and shocked.

'Something's happened to Mum' she said.

'What on earth do you mean?'

'I have to go and identify her again. It looks as if someone has... switched her body or something.'

'What?'

'When the pathologist came to examine her he found she was – well, barely more than a heap of dust and bones. It was as if she had been dead for centuries. It doesn't make sense.'

We just gaped at her.

'But it does' said Vadoma from the sitting room. She came into the kitchen with a smile on her face, Fonso and Esmeralda behind her. 'You must see. Granny is a revenant. She keeps coming back. She was not just ninety years old, she was many centuries old. That's why she was saying 'See you again soon' when she died. Always she comes back.'

'I thought as much' nodded Esmeralda.

'I don't understand any of this, but Mum always did get the last word in' Alison said.

'And the last laugh' I added. 'Come on, let's get that cellar door fixed. We're going to need to sort this place out if we're staying.'

'Who said we were staying?' asked Alison indignantly.

'You don't think Fonso and I did all that clearing up just so someone else can have a peaceful life here, do you?'

'I suppose you win.' She shrugged her shoulders in defeat. 'But how are we going to explain all this? All the empty jars; Reg saw them when they were full. And they'll never solve those murders'.

'Cup of tea, I think' put in Esmeralda.